Art is but one of many passions for me. I believe creativity and imagination requires no formal training and all of us have an artist inside of us. I spent much of my life drawing and painting in traditional ways , but years ago, I found with my computer I could create far more than my skills with a pencil or brush could ever produce. What took me days or weeks by hand , now took hours and allowed me to go places with art I only dreamed of before!

Peter Chilelli

Designer of front cover art

Signatories:

President of The United States of America
President of Russian Federation
Prime Minister of the United Kingdom
President of South Africa
Brotherhood Leader
Prime Minister of Israel
Leader of Hamas
Fatah Leader
Leader of Palestine
President of Iran
President of Syria
Secretary General of the United Nations

International Peace Agreement

for the cessation of all hostilities

Israel , Gaza Strip and other areas

2013

"New World Order "
for the Boundary change
in the
Middle-East

Under the Seal of
The United States of America

Published and Printed by blurb.com
Front cover by Peter Chilelli

The
"European Photo-Book"
collection

Jon Grainge's

Fateful Decision

"Exposed from within a Buried Secret"

The Author

Born in the western suburbs of London Jon saw service as a trainee RAF 'Jet Jockey' before running his own Marine Sales business for many years.
Then following a spell in hotel marketing and Spanish property sales diverted his efforts into writing and photography under the **"European Photo-Book"** collection

This book is a work of **complete fiction** although it is based around the ongoing current political events of **2014**.
None of the characters are real and are the product of the author's extremely vivid imagination. Any resemblance to actual people, either living or dead, is entirely coincidental. No fear or favour is shown to any particular country, person or group that may presently exist.

Fateful Decision

"Exposed from within a Buried Secret"

is a title from
The
"European Photo-Book"
collection
www.blurb.com/user/store/hightrainman

Other titles include:

"Taken from the Dunes"
"Appointment in CAIRO"
"Appointment in DOUZ"
"Appointment with the FAITH"
"A Voice from Heaven"
"Counter-Strike"
"Echoes from a Silent Enemy"
"Appointment in Puerto Banus"

Dedication

I am dedicating this novel to all those poor souls who so tragically lost their lives aboard the ill-fated Malaysian Flight **MH370** that 'disappeared' in the Indian Ocean in early 2014

Jon Grainge

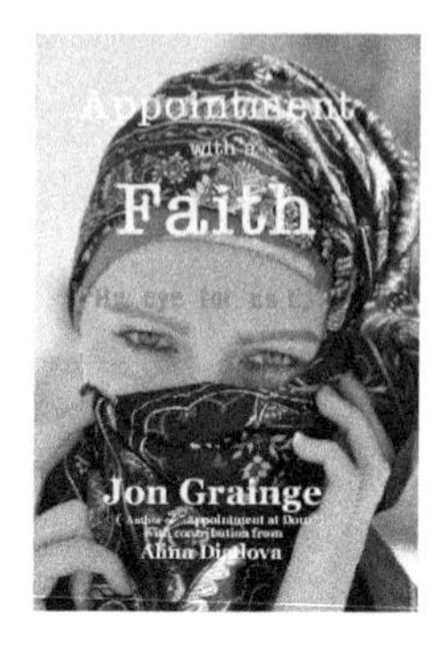

Further:
Action
Adventure
Novel titles
in the collection

Jon Grainge
2014

Preface

The '**Peace Agreement**' that was intended to bring an end to war in the Middle East
mysteriously disappears
with a
British Airways A380 on a flight over Africa.

The implications are profound with President O'Shea mistaking the cause of the disappearance.

A new and more complicated Middle East war develops leading to the rise of a new Caliphate.

Old wounds are opened
but what of the outcome?

PALESTINE:
WEST BANK & GAZA
Under Israeli Occupation
Since 1967
1949 Armistice
(Green Line)
Palestinian Authority
Israeli control
0 10 20 mi
0 10 20 30 km
Lake Tiberias
Tiberias
Haifa
Nazareth
ISRAEL
'Afula
Jenin
Tulkarm
Nablus
Jordan
WEST BANK
JORDAN
Tel Aviv
Ramallah
Jericho
Jerusalem
Bethlehem
Qiryat
Gat
Dead
Sea
Gaza
GAZA
Hebron
Beersheba
EGYPT

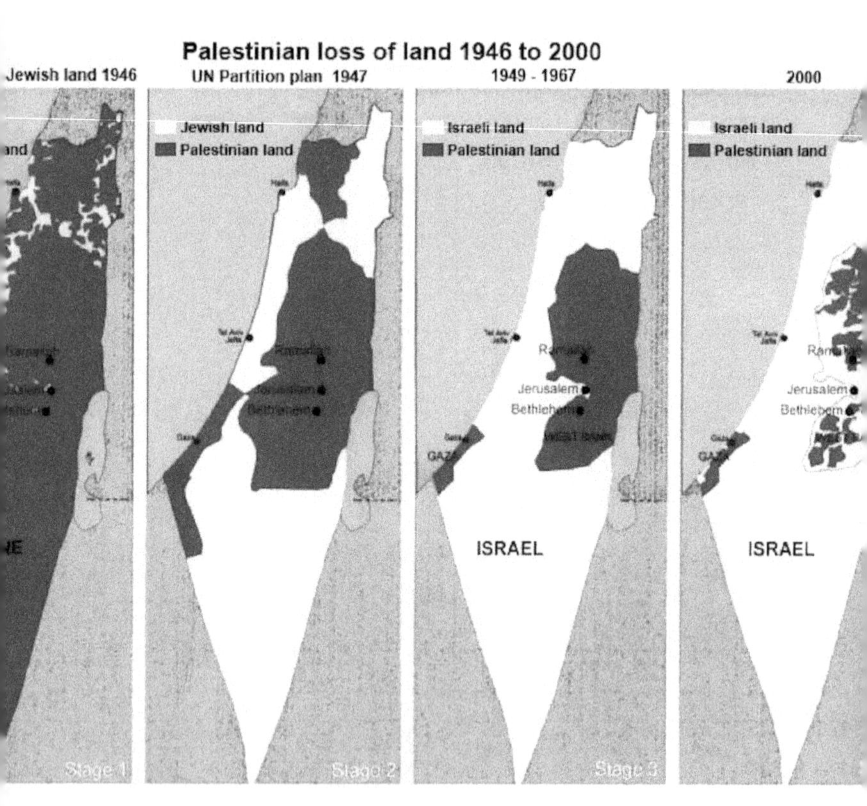
Palestinian loss of land 1946 to 2000
Jewish land 1946
UN Partition plan 1947
1949 - 1967
2000
Jewish land
Palestinian land
Israeli land
Palestinian land
Israeli land
Palestinian land
Jerusalem
Bethlehem
GAZA
ISRAEL
ISRAEL
Stage 1
Stage 2
Stage 3

Main Characters within "Fateful Decision"

Colonel Piratin
Pilot of the D-2
Nasir Mohammed (Mr X)
Brotherhood Leader
Rodriguez Sevilla
Peace Envoy
Dick O'Shea
United States President
Roger Feldman
UK Prime Minister
Zubair Khumalo
South African President
Dimitri Obloff
Russian President
Group Captain Dick Barton
The MI6 Go-Between
Miss Yellowstone
Secretary to Peace Envoy
Jacob Benayoun
Prime Minister of Israel
Gorani
President of Syria
Robert Kuok
UN Secretary-General
Ahmad Habib
Hamas Leader
Mustafar Sawali
Fatah Leader
Adofo Fofana
South African Chief of Staff
President Gorani
President of Syria
President Akbari
President of Iran
Widad Kuttab
Leader of Palestine Front
Douglas Myers
BA Director of Operations

Chapter One

.... "Build-up"

The real trouble started just after the Christmas break of 2012. Most world leaders thought the worst to be over and were about to calculate the damage to their economies following many months of on-the-seat newsflashes throughout the global media including the huge traffic peddled over the social networks. Twitter almost blew a fuse with the incalculable amount of international tweets choking up it's network. Both President Gorani of Syria, who was so keen to quell the bombing on his southern borders in order to concentrate on his inept destruction of the civil rebel uprising in his own country, and Prime Minister Benayoun of Israel had finally, after so many fruitless meetings in Geneva, agreed a ceasefire to the utter devastation of Gaza in his attempt to eliminate the massive Hamas terrorist cell buried deep into Garzan society. The final pressure bought to bear upon Benayoun by the leaderships of the United States, Egypt and Iran plus that of Gorani became too much for him to withstand. The threats of commercial and financial isolation would not be acceptable to either Benayoun or the Israeli people as a whole, especially with an election looming in around eleven months time so having assembled his cabinet and military commanders in the Knesset in Tel Aviv on November 12th 2011, carrying a facial expression that could have reached the floor, he reluctantly informed them to cease all operations against Gaza. The room , stunned with this sudden announcement, had no choice than to agree and so one by one departed to wind down the hostilities.

Within hours silence fell on the battlefield between the two old enemies for the first time in several weeks which allowed the populous of both countries the opportunity to retrieve their dead and afford them proper funerals.

When this news finally arrived at the Cairo headquarters of the Egyptian Brotherhood a sigh of relief could be heard as far south as Aswan. Nasir Mohammed, being the sole undisputed leader of the Sunni Brotherhood and the main instigator of a peace plan had spent many hours in conversations with all parties and was now well satisfied with his efforts.

The forty four year old Imam from Memphis, the ancient Pharonic capitol of Egypt, with his exceptionally dark skin and long black curly beard, stood a good six foot two inches, which is very tall for an Egyptian, and further carried a great deal of authority wherever he travelled. He was an educated man able to converse with no effort in Egyptian, Syrian and English. Throughout his life his love and respect of Islam had never been questioned and often preached the old ways of the famed Kur'an which many in the west saw as a mild form of terrorism. For as long as he could remember he wanted to bring down the military leadership of his country who he saw being decadent towards western ideals with the consequent result in Egypt becoming accepting of so many changes which flew in the face of Kur'an teachings.

It was in the snap election of 2010 following a violent and bloody uprising that stretched across the whole country in which he played a major part, that his Brotherhood suddenly found themselves in power and him as the

legally elected President of Egypt.
Now with the responsibility of the future of Egypt firmly in his hands and those of his closest and most trusted colleagues he set about altering the destiny and direction of Egyptian politics and it's world standing.
Many of his subjects did not agree with his retrograde policies and rearwards approach so once again all was not smooth running in this burning hot and bankrupt country.
However, as he cast his eyes toward Gaza and saw the pounding and devastation being hurled upon them by the might and heavily armed Israel, he took courage and appreciation of his own less suffering internal position.
It had been in the realm of tradition over the past fifty or so years that whenever Israel was moved to invade either Gaza, Palestine or Lebanon it fell to the leadership of Egypt to propose a way to peace or a ceasefire, so to this end Nasir Mohammed, also known as Mr X from the days of when his true identity was only known to those close to his persuasion, had negotiated to this present position of a ceasefire at the November 2011 talks.

With international tempers now somewhat under control it was President O' Shea, whilst sat in the baronial confines of the oval room in the White House, who diplomatically insisted that a comprehensive and all encompassing, long-term international peace agreement be drawn up between Israel and Gaza which would then be ceremoniously signed individually in front of the world's media in a final attempt to bring some prolonged period of peace to the troubled land burning away at the eastern end of the Mediterranean.

The immediate reaction on hearing this idea was concerning to say the least to most of the involved parties concerned, however, following due deliberation and much, much burning of midnight oil in the Knesset, Hamas HQ in Gaza and Nasir's office in Tahrir Square, Cairo it was finally agreed, but, it was Jacob Benayoun that further insisted that the final Peace Agreement containing all the details, maps and concessions be drawn up by the Americans and then signed and witnessed by several other important world leaders first before being presented to each of the four Middle-Eastern countries/groups for their monograms be entered into the annals of history.

Those of Ahmad Habib, the leader of Hamas

in the Gaza Strip, Mustafa Sawali, leader of Fatah in the West Bank, Ali Benal of Lebanese Hezbollah, Widad Kuttab of the Palestinian Front and President Gorani of Syria would be the important signatories.

This was a rather unexpected but understandable request and took a further few days for the final list of proposed world leaders to be agreed upon.
With much concern, heartache and minor horse trading complete the final list of leaders that would be put pen to paper would be:
US President O'Shea,
UK Prime Minister Roger Feldman,
South African President Zubair Khumab,
Russian Federation President Dimitri Obloff,
Iranian President Akbari
and
United Nations Secretary-General Robert Kuok.
These signatures would lie below and be witness to and on the same page as those of Nasir Mohammed of the Egyptian Brotherhood, Prime Minister Jacob Benayoun of Israel, President Gorani of Syria, Ali Benal of Hezbollah, Mustafa Sawali of Fatah and finally that of Ahmad Habib

himself the leader of Hamas.

Once the wording of the agreement had been established it would be drawn up, printed and bound in beautiful leather in Washington and then delivered by the UN Peace Envoy Rodriguez Sevilla to each International Leader in turn for signing before it was finally transported to Cairo for the ceremonious joint signing by Habib, Mohammed, Sawali, Benal and Benayoun. Once completed the Peace Agreement would immediately be flown to New York, escorted by Rodriguez Sevilla, for safe storage in the vaults of the United Nations Headquarters where it would lie for evermore as legal testament to anyone that might wish to break the agreement in the future.
Meanwhile the ceasefire was holding. The pressure and determination for both Israel and Gaza to cease the needless slaughter of thousands of Gazans and occasional Israeli was working and gave the citizens of the narrow ten kilometre wide strip the chance to take in the total devastation that had been inflicted upon their community by the continual air strikes from the Israeli F-16 fighter jets.
Virtually no building in the forty five

kilometre length of Gaza was untouched. Most were just a pile of rubble with personal belongings strewn about the flattened remains with clothes blowing in the chilly winter breeze and pages of books fluttering until there were no more pages to turn but the worst sight that beheld them was the copious quantity of bodies, body parts and streams of blood which brought home the true human cost of their long dispute with their hated neighbour, Israel.

Mr Kumar arrived at what was his home in Nezarim only to find that his third floor apartment was peacefully resting at ground level in a thin, clinging cloud of dust. Scrambling among the breeze blocks throwing them out of his way one by one in his desperate attempt to locate his wife and four children who he suspected were under the rubble. They could still be alive. He had seen the incoming missile that had caused the damage and thought it to be only a small device. His family could still have survived or so he thought!

When he came across the shoe that he recognised to be that of his wife's he collapsed in grief on finding her foot inside. She was dead. It did not take long before both sons and both daughters were

unearthed as they had all taken refuge in the same bedroom seconds before the missile struck.
This was such a typical scene following the horrendous pounding of the last few days. The communal hatred of Israel was all too consuming within the Garzan population but amongst all this devastation and continual propaganda issued by their Hamas 'friends,' an understanding that an end to this continuing war had to be found, which grew stronger by the hour within the civilian population.
It was clear to be seen and heard throughout the strip that living in peace, albeit with possible restrictions, with their neighbour was preferable to this death and destruction. They were tired and Hamas saw this!
The want for a prolonged peace treaty was there for the taking and the reducing support and loyalty for the Hamas way could not be ignored by Habib. To save any degree of enthusiasm for his group's idea of a strict Islamic lifestyle he had to be seen to cooperate and defend the search for a peaceful future in the old Biblical land, hence his agreement to sign the Peace Treaty, at this time.
The hunger for information by the world's

media, beset by the acres of ruins, who conducted their satellite interviews with as many inhabitants as they could in the most effective and dramatic locations such as schools, hospitals, mosques and care centres to highlight their story to their employer's readership and audience.
Poor Mr Kumar had the weight of NBC news descend upon him in his dark hour in their keenness to televise a live feed of his unfortunate demise back to the United States in support of the growing 'stop the war' campaign.
The boss of NBC knew of the need to connect in with the fast growing anti war lobby who had taken to the streets of all the major cities brandishing their placards requiring the armed Civil Guard to be distributed in large numbers to control the mobs.

Across the fields in the cities of Israel a similar voicing of relief was being expelled although in the Knesset an all together different atmosphere prevailed. Whilst the politicians were fully aware of the somewhat lack of result and strength of resolve of Hamas during the massive bombardment of the last few weeks, deep down they wanted the utter destruction of Hamas before any

connection with ISIS in Iraq could be made thus uniting an unholy union of thuggish terrorists stretching right across the Middle-East. But an election was only months away and they wanted to return to power in the forlorn hope that they might finish the job, if the world would let them!
Over the following few days the overall air of calm descended across the entire Middle-East, from Egypt almost to Iraq, although the utter futility of the civil war in Syria still continued unabated and almost forgotten about by the world media. Gorani's intransigence and total disregard against any criticism of his inhuman actions was beginning to bore the global audience. Despite many attempts to bring him to the peace table, all of which ended in failure, his slaughtering of his own but diverse religious people fell from the headlines.
The same could not be said of Iraq itself where the Americans were coming under extreme pressure to act against the ISIS terrorists who were rapidly forging their way towards Baghdad in waves of unspeakable savagery.
Jacob Benayoun and his inner Council were despairing at the perilous thought of a link formatting between ISIS, Hamas, Hezbollah,

Fatah and the Egyptian Brotherhood. Should that happen then it would turn upon the United States and members of NATO to unleash their mighty weaponry upon the Islamic hoards before being committed to place thousands of boots on the ground. The repercussions of all this could further escalate into a Third World War was the fear of the Knesset.

If only they (Israel) could annihilate Hamas then the link could not be made and a further conflict might well be avoided, was the general perception from Tel Aviv.

The drawing up of the most important Middle-East Peace Agreement in modern times began in earnest in the corridors of power, deep in the White House however within the next few days a unusual event would pour oil onto the smoothing waters!

Chapter Two

..."An unforeseen event approaches"

With the huge resources of the American Administration at their disposal, the writers and physical producers of the treaty, took little time in constructing the A3 dossier which consisted of a cover, bound in the finest burgundy Moroccan leather embossed with gold leaf lettering on the front to the effect,

'International Peace Agreement'
Middle-East
2012

enclosing several pages of best vellum containing the script, full coloured representation of each of the signatorics flag and an itemised area for the signatories to impose their marks.
The weighty dossier was further protected by encasing it in it's own plain black presentation box. In all, the package came in at just under a kilo in weight. The designers believed that an agreement of such magnitude should be blessed with the air of importance and authority which they felt the sheer size and weight conveyed.
Escorted by a contingent of fully armed Marines, proudly dressed in their blues and greys, the massive book was delivered from the White House publication office on the
-4 level, to the Oval Office for the first of the signatories to ink in their best signature ...that of Dick O'Shea, the President of the United States of America.
As with true accord to such great events the avalanche of press had been invited to witness the signing. The room lit up with so many flash lights clicking away as the ink from O'Shea's pen took to the vellum.
It was done ; the first of the many signatures was laid to history. The slight figure of the

President rose to his feet and raised his hands for silence,
"Ladies and Gentlemen. It is with great pride that I endorse this Peace Agreement and on behalf of the people of the United States I wish it well on it's inception and obeyance for many years to come."
A round of applause commenced which was allowed to echo around the world through the many television feeds accepted into the White House for this occasion.
O'Shea continued,
"I now hand this agreement over to Rodriguez Sevilla who, as the elected Peace Envoy of the United Nations, will firstly escort it across the pond to London where Prime Minister Feldman and other leaders are awaiting it's arrival before taking it on to Cape Town for President Khumab to sign and then finally over to Cairo for all the Middle-East representatives to finally endorse it's legitimacy. Signor Sevilla I leave this agreement in your tender care."
The exceptionally well dressed Spaniard sat next to President O'Shea now took to his feet,
"Ladies and Gentlemen, Señoras y señores I take possession of this agreement and will henceforth discharge my duty by taking it to Cairo via London and Cape Town. May God

bless it."
Picking up the weighty book he proceeded to depart the Oval Room, with the military escort and his secretary, Miss Yellowstone, following close behind, via the secondary door located to the left of O'Shea.
The audio within the 'room of power' suddenly heightened as each media interviewer directed their questions with vigour at the President.
Meanwhile, some six thousand miles away in the still cool night of Tel Aviv, Jacob Benayoun and his Council sat observing the occasion on the television. The expressions on all their faces gave way to their true reactions .. how long would this accord last? They had been here before; back in 2009 and 2003 when similar but not quite such comprehensive agreements had come and gone; why should this one be any different was the shared Israeli thinking, but they nevertheless lived in hope. Benayoun himself along with the majority of his military advisors were all of the same strategy which was to finish off Hamas completely ..now! which they felt certain would send out a finite warning to all other terrorist groups of the Middle-East not to threaten Israel unless they wished to face the same demise as

Hamas. This would bring peace .. they calculated.
The convoy was expected by the guard detachment at Andrews Air Base who allowed the United Nations envoy and his escort of four hummers through without impediment.
Inside the vast number 5C hanger, situated at the far side of the airfield, the gleaming white/blue twin engined C-37A Gulfstream sat patiently with it's two crew awaiting it's special payload. As Sevilla stepped out of his limo both flight and ground crew immediately stood to attention bringing their hands to the salute.
Having mounted the three integral steps and entered the sumptuous cabin the smartly dressed envoy and his equally smartly attired secretary in her green one piece followed by two of the armed militarymen, was greeted with the smiling faces of the three flight attendants,
" *Good morning sir, welcome aboard Air Force six. As soon as we are airbourne would you both like coffee or cocktails?*" the polite and pristinely turned out purser asked.
"*Hello, I think on this mission it would not be appropriate to abide in alcohol so coffee will do for us both thank you*" and promptly

took his window seat indicating to Miss Yellowstone to sit opposite him. No sooner had Sevilla clicked closed his seat belt the entrance door was slammed shut and the Rolls Royce engines started to whine into life.
It took no more than two minutes for the Captain to complete his flight checks and gain Air Traffic permission to taxi to 09R for an immediate take-off.
This was the first time that the envoy had stepped aboard AF 6 so, whilst taxiing, he took the opportunity to survey the opulence. Normally this aircraft type is fitted out for up to nineteen passengers but this particular aircraft had been heavily modified with mahogany furniture, large leather seats, a twin bedded restroom, comprehensive galley/ bar and an extensive suite of communication equipment which only left seating for up to six passengers.
"Good morning lady and gentlemen. We are about to take-off so please ensure you are seated and buckled up and enjoy the six hour flight to London. Today's purser is Christine who will do everything she can to make your flight enjoyable" came over the speaker system in a deep southern American tone..
As the full fifteen thousand pounds of thrust exited each of the two Rolls engines Sevilla

and Yellowstone clearly felt the acceleration as the speed built up to one hundred and thirty knots at which point the Captain raised the nose to start his climb to his intended trans-Atlantic cruise altitude of thirty three thousand feet.
It soon became apparent to the VIP guests as they admired the early morning view through the windows whilst sipping their delightful Kenco coffee that the aircraft had departed the shores of the United States and was now smoothly cruising high above the blue water of the Atlantic Ocean.

Three thousand two hundred and fifty miles due east of the Gulfstream's present position at 1000hrs whilst crossing the fifty eight degree line of latitude, the next four signatories were readying themselves to close in on the Cabinet Room in London's Whitehall, this being the agreed location for their combined signing of the Peace Agreement to take place.
Dimitri Obloff from the Russian Federation had temporary stayed at his Embassy in Kensington Palace Gardens having decided to grab the opportunity of a short private meeting with the UK Prime Minister at Downing Street before taking the short walk

to the Cabinet Office. President Akbari on the other hand took the liberty of staying at The Dorchester for a couple of night's together with several members of his inner council to savour the delights of London 's hospitality. The last but not least signatory, Robert Kuok who had been in London on UN business anyway took advantage of his chauffeur driven Bentley to visit some old friends in Richmond before he too made his way down Whitehall to the Cabinet Office.

"Excuse me sir, we have medallions of lamb with sauté potatoes and a selection of fresh vegetables for a light lunch which should be ready in about half an hour. Would that be to your liking?" asked the purser in such a pleasant voice.
"Great. Could that come with some freshly squeezed orange juice as well?" requested Sevilla.
"Of course sir and for you as well madam?" she asked turning toward Miss Yellowstone.
"Thank you ,yes."
At this point Rodriguez suggested to Miss Yellowstone that she use the restroom for a couple of hours sleep after dinner as he was going to stay up and continue with some work for the remainder of the flight. She

agreed and was grateful of the suggestion.
The hours quietly slipped by as the Gulfstream drew closer and closer to UK territorial waters. Miss Yellowstone had been fast asleep for the past three and a half hours before the purser was instructed to wake her, Sevilla was nearing the end of his report and the security men were rousing from their forty winks.
On the flight deck preparation was being made for their arrival at Northolt Airfield,
" Northolt radar. This is Gulfstream AF6 routing from Washington. Presently at Flight Level 35 over RT1" spoke the Captain into his headset.
"Gulfstream AF6 this is Northolt. Good evening sir. You are expected. Continue your heading and descend to FL 25. No traffic in your path" came the response.
"Lady and Gentlemen we are about to commence our descent into London Northolt. Please ensure you are seated and strapped in. Thank you" rang through the speaker system in Christine's best voice.

The control tower at Northolt, located some ten miles to the west of London which served only diplomatic and senior military traffic, rang down to the senior chauffeur and informed him of the imminent arrival of the Peace Envoy. The two Jaguar XJ's immediately started and positioned themselves on the arrival zone, engines still ticking over in order to provide a warm interior environment for it's occupants on this chilly winter's evening.

The Gulfstream gently touched down on the threshold of 07R in the cool evening air before engaging reverse thrust reducing speed down to a gentle taxy. The Captain, directed by the 'follow me' car and having completed his after landing checks proceeded to taxy towards the arrival zone and the awaiting 'official' cars.
With a slight dipping of the nose as the brakes were applied the Gulfstream came to a halt shortly followed by the winding down of the Rolls Royce turbines and the opening of the cabin door.
The two security guards alighted first and swept the immediate area for any possible concerns before signalling for the Envoy and his secretary to safely descend the steps and enter the first of the two Jaguars. This level of guest and importance of the visit did not require the use of passports or a security search of baggage.

" Good evening sir and madam. Welcome to the UK. We will now be driving you to Whitehall for your meeting with the Prime Minister and returning back here afterwards" the lead chauffeur informed the diplomats.
"Excellent. I will keep this bag in the cabin with me" Sevilla pointed out not wanting to be parted from the most historic of documents for even a second.
Once the passengers were securely inside, the two car convoy sped off through the main gate where four police on motorbikes had been waiting to escort the two Jaguars through any London traffic, onto the A4 and headed towards central London with all haste.

Everything was progressing nicely on schedule towards finalising the legitimacy of the Agreement: the British Prime Minister and his illustrious overseas colleagues had all successfully gathered in the Cabinet Room, the South African President had arranged his stay in Cape Town and the representatives of the Islamic factions were either in situ or in transit to Cairo. What could go wrong?

The evening streets of central London were congested with the usual mid-week traffic as the convoy entered Knightsbridge encountering the late night shoppers and revellers, however as the police motorcyclists responded by engaging their blue lights and excruciatingly loud sirens the traffic eased out of the way. The bright lights of Harrods slipped past on the the right,

"Just wish we had had the time to pop in there for a few goodies" remarked Miss Yellowstone who had heard so much about this famous store yet never had the time to visit from her native Canada.

"Could drop you off now and pick you up on the way back if you want" offered Sevilla.

"Nice thought but somewhat unprofessional I feel sir" she replied bending around to watch the shop disappear behind their progress

"Yes you are right as usual Yellowstone. So glad you are with me" the Envoy uttered under his breath. Not being the most congenial of Spaniards to come out of Madrid the mid sixty year old never appreciated others pointing out his inadequacies. Some said, behind the closed doors of Washington, that he should never

have been selected as the UN representative for this assignment but O'Shea had faith in his choice.
"We are just passing Buckingham Palace sir and after driving down the Mall I will be turning into Whitehall so should have you at the Cabinet Rooms in about four minutes" the chauffeur informed his important passengers.
Expecting their arrival having previously been informed by security at Northolt, the duty police from the Diplomatic Protection Group were in evidence at the convoy's arrival to hold back the hoards of press and journalists gathered on the pavement.
Sevilla stepped out and was immediately hit on the head by a flying custard tart sending him into a protective stoop. Instinctively the police manhandled the middle-eastern woman to the floor,
"Long live Hamas! No peace!" she screamed and screamed as the three constables carried her away.
"*This way sir and Madam*" the Inspector uttered in an deep British voice of authority,
"Sorry about that incident but not everyone in this multi-cultural society here sings of one accord!" he continued.
Entering the the main room the Envoy was

greeted with an array of officials sat around the three leaders he recognised.
Roger Feldman stood and walked across to Sevilla,
"Welcome Rodriquez. I hope you had a pleasant trip. I see you have the agreement with you so let's not waste time., put it on the table and we will all sign" instructed the PM,
" I hope you do not mind but a few members of the press have been invited to record the event" he went on to say.
The first to endorse the document was Prime Minister Feldman closely followed by Dimitri Obloff and finally completed by President Akbari. No more than twenty minutes had passed for the ceremony to be completed amidst the flashlights. It was done. The ink from the Montblanc fountain pen duly blotted and dried, it was time for the UN Envoy and his secretary to leave and make their way to Cape Town to keep the appointment with Ahmad Habib's good friend, President Khumab, whose ratification of the agreement was insisted upon by the Hamas leader.
Having just spent several hours in the confines of a small aircraft crossing the Atlantic without any sleep, Sevilla was showing signs of tiredness which came to the

attention of Feldman who then suggested that he and Miss Yellowstone stay as his guests for the night in a London hotel and depart early the following morning. Whilst Señor Sevilla fully appreciated the gesture he had a timetable to maintain in order to meet up with President Khumab before he departed back to Johannesburg to attend his daughters wedding on the 14th, but nevertheless thanked the Prime Minister for his consideration. The remaining unused bed aboard the jet would have to suffice for the eleven hour flight down to South Africa.
With the formalities fully completed, the Peace Agreement safely back in it's box and nestling under the arm of it's guardian, Rodriguez bid farewell to the assembled dignitaries before making his withdrawal back to his Jaguar closely escorted by Roger Feldman.
A firm handshake from Feldman before taking his (Sevilla) seat in the XJ closed the London commitment for the Spanish Peace Envoy who was now looking forward to a nap in the back of the car during the drive back to Northolt.

Meanwhile back at the airfield the C-37A had been refuelled to the brim, including the fitted five hundred gallon reserve tank specially fitted to the AF Gulfstream fleet enabling long distance journeys without having to refuel in non-cooperative countries and a crew change arranged for the long haul across the African continent.

Allowing himself to fall into a deep sleep Sevilla once more took to the air whilst the new fresh crew navigated the Gulfstream over Madrid, Marrakesh and Bamako and then over Cote D'Ivoire, across a section of the Atlantic before entering Namibian airspace and onto Cape Town on the western seaboard of South Africa. Miss Yellowstone had the luxury of her executive seat to snatch forty or maybe sixty winks!
This was to be a long leg down to the southern hemisphere which had to be carefully and economically flown by Captain Bailey in order to avoid a refuel en-route. This had to be the furthest any Gulfstream had flown non-stop.

The blood red morning sun creeping up from the oceanic horizon was a sure sign of yet another beautiful hot day with deep blue skies over Table Mountain. Khumab rose from his bed, threw open the shutters of his third floor Presidential suite in the fabulous Mount Nelson Hotel to reveal the panoramic view of Table Bay. There was a knock at the door,

"Enter!" Khumab shouted in his usual booming voice.

President Zubair Khumab, a flamboyant larger than life character, had been in office for several years and the stability and prosperity that he had brought to South Africa since the demise of apartheid had made him a popular figure, although he had his enemies. Originally from Bloemfontein he entered public life as a local councillor and worked his way through the African National Combine only to be elected as it's leader in 2008, then with the win in the 2009 General Election, by default he became the first black President of South Africa.

He stood for no nonsense from those who opposed his policies but nevertheless was a fair and honourable man.

"I have your breakfast sir. Eggs with tomatoes on toast" the maid informed her President.

"Put it on the table and ask General Fofana to come and see me here at 10am" he replied with a touch of arrogance in his tone.

"Very well sir, 10am" the timid maid

repeated and departed the room to seek out Fofana .

The Gulfstream was on schedule having entered Namibian airspace over Khorixas and further cleared for a southerly heading of 175 degrees by Windhoek Control.
Sevilla was suddenly awakened by a bout of severe turbulence followed by loud reverberations from the speaker system,
"Good Morning sir. This is Captain Bailey. Sorry about the rough ride but this is due to the morning heat rising from the desert below. I would strongly suggest the use of seat belts. We are over Namibia and about to commence our shallow descent into South African airspace. I anticipate arrival at Ysterplaat Air Base in about forty five minutes."
The intensity of the turbulence increased to the point that Bailey requested from Windhoek a more rapid descent and alteration of course in an attempt to mitigate the uncomfortable ride. They agreed but the violence grew worse as the Gulfsream encountered a severe wind shear and instantly lost two thousand feet in altitude sending the unbuckled Envoy to the ceiling before crashing back to the bed,

"What the fuck!" he shouted in his natural tongue for all to hear. The violence continued for another twenty or so seconds .. then ceased as suddenly as it had appeared. Now the ride was smooth but the aircraft's height was now down to FL 20 (twenty thousand feet).
After filing an information report to Windhoek Control the co-pilot made his announcement to the passengers,
"This is your co-pilot Lieutenant Logan speaking. We do apologise for that but the weather radar gave us no indication of such a wind shear. I do hope everyone is ok. We are now sorted and back on course albeit at a lower height."
With his attire and nerves re-evaluated Sevilla made his appearance in the cabin only to be greeted by Caroline (the new purser) standing outside his bedroom door.
"Good morning sir. Sorry about that. I am afraid to say that the cooked breakfast is now unavailable but we can muster some toast and preserves. Shall I get you a band-aid for that cut on your forehead?"
"No problem, that's fine. I never really liked flying , now I hate it!" he replied feeling for the trickle of blood ousing from the small

flesh wound atop his left eye.
Miss Yellowstone, also recomposed, had had the foresight to have kept her seatbelt locked whilst she snoozed throughout the flight so had suffered no undue setbacks,
"Good morning sir. Only toast for breakfast then!" she remarked.
"Afraid so, no doubt President Khumab will be able to oblige us later on."

The huge black Presidential Mercedes limousine drew up, together with an escort of no less than twenty police motorcycles, under the voluminous portico of the Mount Nelson. The somewhat untidily dressed driver got out and made his way into reception to take up his position by the reception desk to await the appearance of his important passengers.
The minutes ticked by as the long hand on the hotel's central grandfather clock passed five.
"Why is the man always late !" the chauffeur mumbled quietly to himself. Another ten minutes passed, then coming down the marble stairway was the formidable figure of President Khumab accompanied by his
Chief of Staff General Fofana in his full military uniform, medals included.

Not often did Fofana appear in public. He was normally resolved to remain in the background and let his President hog the limelight but on this important and very public ceremony of the signing, which was to be transmitted across the globe, he wanted to receive his due media credit.
"You know we are going to Ysterplaat don't you?" remarked Khumab to the chauffeur who had acknowledged his sighting of the two descending the stairway.
"Of course Mr President. The Officers Mess to be precise " replied the chauffeur.
The extensive motorcade departed the hotel main gates onto Table Bay Boulevard to embark on the short twenty minute journey to the Air Base.

"Ysterplaat Control good morning sir. This is Gulfstream AF6 inbound. Present location two hundred kilometres to your north on a heading of 170 degrees and level at FL20."
"AF6 this is Ysterplaat. Good morning sir Continue your approach for runway 20L. You are cleared for descent to FL 15 " was the reply.
All was proceeding well until Logan noticed a brief surging of the starboard engine being

displayed on the central gauge. It rose from the usual descent setting of forty percent power up to sixty five for a sporadic five seconds before settling back to the correct setting once more. Having pointed this out to Captain Bailey they both eventually conceded that as everything was now running correctly the surge would be ignored and just put down to an unstable airflow passing through the engine.

"AF6 you are now twenty miles from base . Alter heading to 185 degrees and descend to two thousand five hundred feet. Wind 010 5 kts. Advise runway in sight."

"AF6 wildo."

Once again, albeit with a different pair of hands on the stick, the Gulfstream gently touched down on terra ferma and engaged a modicum of reverse thrust before slowly taxiing to the dispersal pad. There was no reception committee or guard of honour in attendance for the alighting Envoy and his secretary, merely a single open jeep and driver who had the respect of offering a salute in welcome.

The fresh morning heat was a welcome to Sevilla after the continual air conditioned environment of the last few hours. It reminded him of the summers back home in

Madrid.

Turning to the driver as the jeep rounded the corner into the car park of the Officers Mess, Miss Yellowstone asked if the Envoy could be directed to the nearest washroom for a shave and brush up before meeting with the President.

"Of course sir, just follow me" replied the driver as he parked the jeep and led the way into the Mess.

Suitably refreshed and reunited with his secretary the Envoy was escorted by the driver to the main reception room at the end of the corridor in which President Khumab and General Fofana were happily imbibing in coffee and biscuits,

"Ah! it must be Signor Sevilla with the agreement good morning welcome. Come and partake in coffee." greeted Khumab,

"May I introduce General Fofana my Chief of Staff."

"Good morning Mr President, General. This is my secretary Miss Yellowstone." Immediately upon casting his eyes upon the Canadian Fofana's eyes lit up! He had ideas and was used to getting his way!

"President Khumab, as you know it was the express will of Mr Habib that you endorse this agreement but before doing so might it

be possible to have a little breakfast? Long story but we were unable to eat on the jet" Sevilla asked.
"Why of course. General will you arrange for a full spread for our guests please and further tell the press we will be another hour" Khumab commanded of Fofana.
"Very well Mr President."
A full stomach sat well with Sevilla as he walked alongside the South African President into the room allocated for the public signing of the document he carried. The simple ceremony itself took just a few minutes but the consequent press conference took a lot longer. Both Khumab and Fofana relished any opportunity to be in the spotlight especially when broadcast around the internet.
With another rather flamboyant signature securely inked in on the agreement the time for the United Nations representatives to depart on the final leg of their mission to Cairo, had arrived. In a last minute attempt to gain as much kudos from his involvement with a peace settlement in the Middle-East, Khumab insisted that he join the duo on their car trip back to the Gulfstream but using his Mercedes. The press, hungry for media footage, followed either on foot or by

their personal transport.
The C-37A had remained in bay 7 during the three and a half hour period of it's passenger's absence and apart from another re-fuel, galley re-stock and interior valet all remained the same. The pilots exchanged seats whilst the cabin staff and security men took advantage on the short break for some kip and if the truth be known so did the flight crew.
Being the 'film star' to the end the precariously portly President mounted the aircraft entry steps , put his arm around the surprised Envoy in the doorway and faced them both toward the press for some dramatic PR photo opportunities.
Hand shakes complete, formalities over with Khumab back beside his black car with the General, the Gulfstream door closed. The Rolls engines burst into life,
"Ysterplaat Tower this is AF6 requesting permission to taxy" spoke Logan who was now the nominated captain for this onward leg to Cairo.
"AF6. You are clear to taxy to 20L. Surface wind 180 6 kts. Your flight plan routing via Windhoek, Kinshasa and Khartoum to Cairo is approved. After lift off climb to and maintain FL 20 on 005 degrees. Good day

sir" replied the African controller.
Gradually Logan opened the throttles for a slow taxy to the threshold of 20 knowing full well that the glow of the press was upon his every move.
Full take-off checks complete, clearance for take-off obtained, the seat belt announcement made and with the President and his entourage waving goodbye from the dispersal pad, Captain Logan threw the throttles fully forward. The aircraft accelerated rapidly passing 20, 60, 80 kts. All was going well as Logan was about to pull the stick back at V1 (take-off speed, which is
110 kts for the Gulfstream) when an almighty bang was clearly heard from within the cabin. Immediately Logan saw the starboard engine RPM percentage dial dramatically reduce to zero. To be selected to fly any of the Presidential Air Force Squadron the pilots have to be specially selected and must hold the highest of flying ability and to this end the lightning reaction of Captain Logan closed the two throttles and applied the brakes only microseconds before the Gulfstream was committed to flight at VR. Smoke poured from the brake linings as both pilots depressed the brake pedals. The press and entourage stood shocked and stunned in

a helpless scene of awe as they observed the flames issuing from where the engine was. With an equal reaction the two duty fire engines burst into life and headed toward the runway at full speed.

The aircraft came to an abrupt halt and again with equal professionalism the three cabin crew threw open the cabin door and inflated the emergency escape slide before ushering the passengers, one by one, to jump onto the slide having first removed their shoes.

Captain Logan was the last to evacuate the Gulfstream having shut down all fuel and electrical systems, which coincidently was when the foam started to pour onto the burning starboard rear of the fuselage.

From the dispersal pad the scene looked tragic as amidst the clouds of smoke and foam appeared the nine figures, led by one of the security team grasping the hand of his Envoy boss whilst running towards the relative safety of a grassed banking.

Not wishing to be either absent or oblivious to the unfolding events Khumab commanded his driver to immediately take the Mercedes over to the bank and bring the Envoy and his team back to the dispersal pad to discuss the situation and how he might be of help.

As the fire crew had things under control both

flight crew walked back and surveyed the rear of their aircraft as best they could through the remains of the dripping foam. Parts of the starboard engine cowling were missing allowing exposure of the turbine blades. It was Captain Bailey who offered the first appraisal,

"Seen this before on a DC-9. It was found that a turbine blade had failed and broke up. Could be what happened here. In any event it's a replacement engine. Better go and inform Mr Sevilla but looks like we are going to be stuck here in the sun for a few days."

On hearing his report Sevilla had a situation on his hands; how was he to get to Cairo by the following day for his appointment with the Islamic faction leaders?

This incident was a scoop for the press, most of whom were frantically engaged in uploading photographic data to their relevant editors on their laptops hoping for a front page.

"Come let's go back into the mess and analyse the position" insisted Khumab beckoning his driver to open the car doors.

"That would be a good idea sir. Best we get out of the limelight here" Sevilla agreed.

Chapter Three

..."One thing after another"

The Officers Mess provided an oasis of tranquillity from the ensuing chaos outside for some serious thought on how to address the present situation.

After considerable discussions and suggestions amongst the somewhat stunned and nervous gathering, it was the normally quiescent and cooperative Miss Yellowstone who came forward with the obvious solution, should it be possible to enact,

" Gentlemen, gentlemen may I just ask a

question; is there a commercial flight going to Cairo from any nearby airport?"
Immediately Fofana spoke forth,
"Of course such an obvious question. Only a woman could think that sensibly" and withdrew his smart phone from it's holster and searched flight enquiries at Cape Town International.
With glee in his eye and a smirk on his extremely large full featured face the General offered his successful finding,
"I have it! There is a British flight going direct to Cairo in two and a half hours time at 13.15 hrs."
"Very well General that is good news get onto British Airways now and secure two first class seats " Khumab commanded.
At this point Sevilla rapidly interjected,
" Better make that four seats General. I will require security to come with me and put the booking down to the UN account, my card is easily sufficient cover it."
With not a moment to loose Khumab offered the Spaniard, Canadian and the two Americans the use of his Mercedes limousine and driver plus the police escort to convey them all to the airport with all haste whilst he and Fofana would take the opportunity of a brief lunch in the Officers Mess and await the

return of his car.
Before popping back to the crippled Gulfstream in order to retrieve their personal possessions and having once again completed his farewell and thanks to Khumab, Sevilla politely requested that President Khumab personally contact Nasir Mohammed in Cairo at his earliest opportunity and inform him of the slight change in plan and his (Sevilla) arrival time into Cairo. Khumab agreed.
It was a relatively quiet January scene at Cape Town International as the convoy drew up outside the main departure terminal. What people there were going about their routine business stopped in their tracks to observe and ascertain the identity of the dignitary that had the occasion to arrival in such style.
Not wanting to attract any undue publicity for this unscheduled arrival which would eventually shed further light on the demise of one of the Presidential aircraft, Sevilla and his party beat a hasty retreat into the terminal and headed for the British Airways lounge where a sanctuary of peace and quiet might exist.
"Good morning sir. Might I be of assistance?" asked the uniformed

receptionist.
Miss Yellowstone took over the conversation,
"This is Señor Rodriguez Sevilla of the United Nations. We have four first class seats on the Cairo flight."
The receptionist briefly scrolled her desk computer,
"Ah yes Mr Sevilla, Unfortunately there was only one first class seat available so we booked you all into Cub World Class, I hope that will be ok?"
"Fine as long as we get there!" Sevilla interrupted.
"Great sir. You will be boarding in around thirty minutes time from gate 12A. It happens to be the first Airbus 380 on this route and you should arrive at 23.30hrs, meanwhile please enjoy the club's facilities" the receptionist advised.
It was at the point when they were about to help themselves to a coffee from the guest bar that the senior of the two man security team pointed out that they were still armed! This pre-empted Miss Yellowstone to slip back over to the receptionist and very carefully advise her of this status.
Without hesitation she dived to the floor as per the BA training manual instruction ,
" It's ok Miss we are Government agents

there is no cause for alarm" informed Miss Yellowstone leaning over the counter.
Once all was explained then the receptionist calmed down and proceeded to advise that the police would have to come and remove the weapons for storage in the hold of the aircraft.
Everything now was practically back on schedule and safe in the knowledge that there would be an official car to greet them at Cairo and take them to the Four Seasons Hotel on the banks of the Nile, Sevilla began to settle back into his normal relaxed condition again to the point where his deep brown Spanish eyes began to close. Suddenly without warning came the announcement,
"Would all passengers on flight BA 4674 to Cairo make their way to gate 12A for immediate embarkation."
For Miss Yellowstone this was a treat as she had never been on a jumbo sized aircraft before let alone this huge , gleaming new A380 which was known to be the largest airliner in the sky. With it's two floor levels she was totally overwhelmed as she climbed the staircase to Club World Class. Fortunately, all four had been seated close together.
Soon all the passengers were aboard and on

PORTUGAL
SPAIN
ITALY
BULGARIA
ALBANIA
GREECE
GEORGIA
ARMENIA
TURKEY
CYPRUS
SYRIA
LEBANON
ISRAEL
JORDAN
IRAQ
Mediterranean Sea
Str. of Gibraltar
Casablanca
Rabat
MOROCCO
Marrakech
Madeira (PORT.)
Algiers
Tunis
TUNISIA
Tripoli
Alexandria
Cairo
Suez
El Aaiún
WESTERN SAHARA (S.A.D.R.)
ALGERIA
LIBYA
EGYPT
L. Nasser
Red Sea
Nile
MAURITANIA
Nouakchott
MALI
Timbuktu
Niger
NIGER
CHAD
Port Sudan
Khartoum
ERITREA
SUDAN
Blue Nile
White Nile
Bamako
Ouagadougou
BURKINA FASO
Niamey
L. Chad
N'Djaména
DJIBOUTI
GUINEA
SIERRA LEONE
CÔTE D'IVOIRE
GHANA
TOGO
BENIN
NIGERIA
Abuja
Benue
Addis Ababa
Monrovia
Yamoussoukro
LIBERIA
Abidjan
Cape Palmas
Accra
Lomé
Porto Novo
Lagos
CENTRAL AFRICAN REPUBLIC
Bangui
CAMEROON
Yaoundé
Malabo
EQUATORIAL GUINEA
Gulf of Guinea
Ubangi
UGANDA
L. Albert
Kampala
KENYA
L. Turkana
SÃO TOME & PRINCIPE
Libreville
GABON
CONGO
ZAÏRE
Zaïre
Kigali
RWANDA
L. Victoria
Nairobi
Bujumbura
BURUNDI
Brazzaville
Kinshasa
CABINDA (ANGOLA)
Dodoma
TANZANIA
ATLANTIC
Luanda
ANGOLA
MALAWI
L. Nyasa
OCEAN
ZAMBIA
Lilongwe
Lusaka
Zambezi
L. Kariba
Cape Fria
Cunene
MOZAMBIQUE
Harare
ZIMBABWE
NAMIBIA
BOTSWANA
Limpopo
Windhoek
Gaborone
Pretoria
Maputo
Johannesburg
Mbabane
SWAZILAND
Vaal
Maseru
LESOTHO
Durban
Orange
SOUTH AFRICA
Cape Town
Port Elizabeth
Cape of Good Hope
10° West of Greenwich 0° East of Greenwich 10°
20°
30°
40°

looking around Miss Yellowstone thought it to be a full flight. So many people, how the hell could this lot get into the air she thought to herself as she sat back and settled into the massive but so comfortable seat. She did notice a profuse sweating on the male passenger on the opposite aisle but thought little of it..maybe he was just nervous. The four gigantic Rolls Royce Trent engines started and push back commenced,

"Ladies and Gentlemen welcome on-board this British Airways Airbus A380 to Cairo. My name is Leanne and I will be your purser on this our inaugural flight to Cairo

from South Africa. Flight time will be seven hours so sit back, relax and enjoy the flight."
Within minutes the huge gleaming white A380 with it's special African colour stream stood ready to power up at the end of runway 30L .
"Speedbird 4674 you are cleared for take-off. Surface wind 165 8 kts. Good day sir."
The captain plunged the four throttles fully forward as the A380 required full power to get airbourne in the ninety degree South African heat. 70, 90, 120 kts and the great white bird rose gracefully into the air. Undercarriage up and away it flew on the

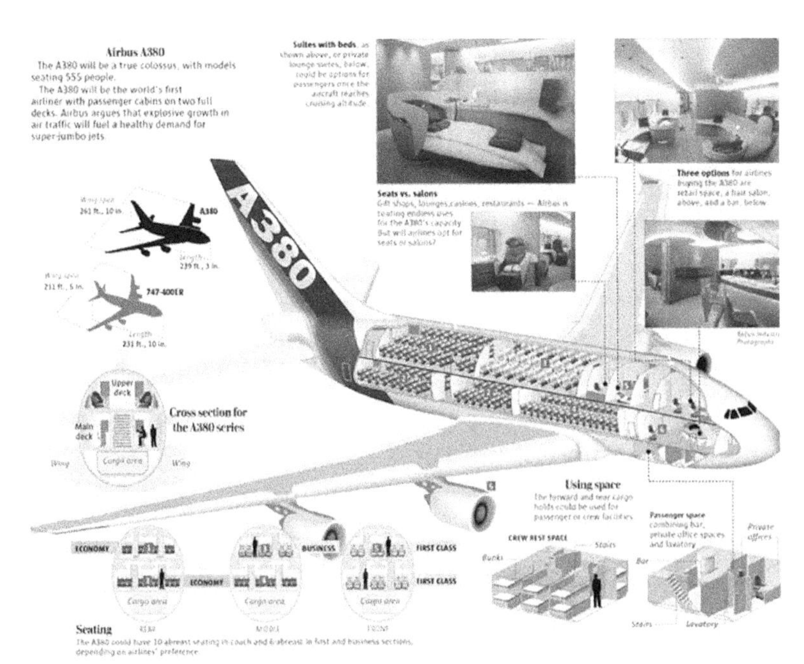

first leg to Windhoek.
Settling down for the long flight Sevilla suggested that Miss Yellowstone order a round of drinks for them both and coffee's for the security guys.
"Make mine a glass of Rioja and you order what you want Clarice." This was the first time in the four years that they had worked together that he had called her by her first name! Maybe the relaxed environment of the moment aboard the new jet liner had softened the married Sevilla's brain.
The aircraft levelled and Captain Maltravers reduced the power setting to attain a cruise of Mach 0.75 (575 MPH). The flight attendants on the second deck began the first of the many services with the lunch trolley but up on the first level the impressive menus were being distributed to the passengers.
"Oh my word I am so hungry sir I could eat a horse. Just look at the menu: Roast beef, Chicken, Salmon, Lamb ....arh and the deserts! I will have the chicken and tart. How about you sir?" asked Miss Yellowstone as she sipped her gin and tonic supporting a side garnish of lemon.
"Make it the beef, Miss Yellowstone. That will do me fine."
Forward in the flight deck the two pilots were

busy changing communication frequencies and inputting the computer. Now leaving South African airspace it was time to contact Windhoek,

"Windhoek radar this is Speedbird 4674 en-route Kinshasa VOR at FL 35 on a heading of 350 degrees" Captain Maltravers informed the controller sat in the darkened room at Windhoek Radar. A few seconds passed,

"Speedbird 4674 this is Windhoek. Good afternoon sir. I have you on scope. Continue on your flight plan."

Once the Airbus was in the overhead of the Windhoek VOR beacon the on-board navigation computer altered the aircraft's course to 345 degrees on it's quest to pick up Kinshasa VOR.

Once again the ground radar made contact with the A380,

"Speedbird 4674 you are leaving Windhoek radar. Contact Luanda radar on 145.9. Good day sir."

"Windhoek . Luanda 145.9 many thanks good day to you, 4674 out. "

In the cabin lunch was now over with most of the passengers dozing off into a sleep.

"Speedbird 4674. Good Afternoon." no reply.

"Speedbird 4674. This is Luanda radar. Do you read me?" No reply.
"Speedbird 4674 en-route to Cairo from Cape Town. This is Luanda radar. I have you on my scope (radar) at FL 35 on a heading of 345 degrees. Do you read me, over."
"Speedbird 4674 come in please I am not receiving you, Speedbird 4674." Nothing just a feint hiss in the controller's headset.

In Cairo the leaders of the various Islamic factions had amassed in Mohammed's head office in El-Tahrir Square. Overlooking the famous pink painted Cairo Museum from his eight floor suite of offices in Meret Basha Str the tall Mr X, as he was formerly known, stood at the window tapping his finger, the one adorned with the most fabulous deep turquoise Lapis stone ring, on the sill whilst the remaining leaders, namely those of Hamas, Hezbollah, Syria and Fatah sat in relative silence around the huge round mahogany table.
It was all too obvious to the Brotherhood

leader, now Egyptian President, that his fellow Sunni friends were not overly happy with the conditions stated in the Peace Agreement that they were all about to sign as soon as the UN Envoy arrived from South Africa.

All were agreed that the killings, the massacres, the executions had to stop and that the key to a successful economic and political growth in each of their domains would only be achievable if peace reined throughout the Middle-East but the recognition of Israel's continued power and presence in the Middle-East did not sit well with any of them, especially Ahmad Habib of Hamas who had lost so much dignity in the recent hostilities. However, the power and control that Mohammed waved within the Islamic community had managed to convince them of the sense of an agreement. It would not be till later, months after the agreement had been signed, that Mohammed would eventually announce to the world of his intention to build another Suez Canal alongside the existing one to bolster his country's revenue and of course his own power base. For this to happen he needed long term peace in the area and confidence that more and more foreign ships would be

encouraged to use it when completed.
"My friends, tomorrow will be an historic day. In this room will sit old enemies of the past. Jacob Benayoun will be here as will the United Nations representative. We will all put our marks to the document and we must hold our word. It will be difficult, we all know that, but there is no other way. Allah be praised" Mohammed preached to the gathered as he gazed from the window toward Tahrir Square where so many of his followers had recently died in the 'Spring' uprising.

"Speedbird 4674, Speedbird 4674 come in . Do you read me! Do you read me!" shouted the concerned controller. Still silence. It was now time to inform the Duty Controller Director of the degrading situation. It had now been around twenty minutes since the acknowledged handover from Windhoek and still no contact with the aircraft.
The Controller Director quickly made his way across the darkened room to his controllers booth and attempted two further communications with Speedbird 4674 .. no luck!
"Could be a total radio failure aboard the plane" the controller offered as an

explanation.
"Possibly but we must keep trying. At least we have a return on the scope so it's still in the air! I will inform Kinshasa and British Airways of the situation" replied the Director and promptly returned to his office. No sooner than he lifted the telephone receiver when an almighty shout was clearly heard across the whole centre,
"It's gone, the signature has gone Jesus Christ it's gone!"

The Director ran back to the scope and sure enough the green translucent transponder information about the location, height and direction of Speedbird 4674 that had been displayed on the scope had completely disappeared. Normally this would indicate that the aircraft had crashed. Every airliner, whilst airbourne, in the world transmits a continual array of technical information which shows up on the radar screen of any tracking station. It would be of the utmost stupidity and a complete breach of navigation law for any aircraft captain to switch this transponder off.
The British Airways A380 was the latest generation of airliner and was fully able to be interrogated by the ground ADS-B system (Automatic Dependent Surveillance-Broadcast)

which enables all GPS information gathered aboard the aircraft from overhead satellites to be transmitted onto the global Flightradar 24 receivers which in turn pass it on to the tracking radar scopes. Most of the world had a copious quantity of these F24 receivers which allow a very precise coordination of the aircraft's position, however, Africa only has a few resulting in a relatively inaccurate readout ..but there is still a readout! When that readout disappears off the scope it can only mean one of three possible situations: Either the aircraft transponder has been switched off or the aircraft has experienced a total and complete electrical failure or the aircraft has crashed!

The first procedure to follow with an expected crash is to inform the airline, the destination airport and alert all the emergency services to commence an immediate search in the aircraft's last known position which in the case of Speedbird 4674 was an area within a thirty or so mile radius of the Angolan town of Huambo.

The Director Controller made contact with the Angolan authorities and requested that they initiate a search for the missing Airbus having given them the rough search area. He then put a call through to the airline's Director of Operations at Heathrow in the United Kingdom.

On hearing the dreadful news that their new pride and joy had gone down in southern Africa filled Douglas Myers with immense sadness and shock but not wishing this to cloud his judgement firstly informed his CEO, Sir Leonard Foley, before arranging his own flight down to Cape Town to oversee the rescue operation. Sir Leonard went puce in the face with a mixture of rage and embarrassment on receiving the call from Myers as he now had the unpleasant task of calling a press conference at Heathrow in advance of the unavoidable onslaught about to descend on him by the world's media. At this point he was not aware of the important passenger sitting in Club World of Speedbird 4674 or more importantly what he was carrying in his briefcase!
The nearest airbase to the anticipated crash site was that of Kuito Air Base, not a huge base but it supported a few aircraft that could be of use. On receiving the upsetting communication from Luanda the base commander ordered all his fleet, which consisted of three Lockheed C-130's, four Antonov-12's and two Antonov-72's into the air with the utmost haste. He , Colonel

Abyara, also commanded that his personal Gazelle helicopter be readied for immediate flight. No way was he going to miss out on this possible opportunity to upgrade his rank in the event of a successful recovery.

The Airport Director at Cairo International was devastated to hear from his opposite number at Cape Town and took a couple of hours before deciding upon his best action which was to request a copy of the passenger manifest from British Airways to ascertain the names of any VIP's or dignitaries that might have been on-board. He fully realised that it was the responsibility of the airline to inform it's passengers but if an Egyptian of 'position' was included in the list then he would approach the relevant authority before the airline.
He would not advise the general public by tannoy and arrivals notification of the loss until the very last moment just in case the aircraft miraculously appeared.
On examining the manifest the name Rodriguez Sevilla (United Nations representative) caught his eye. Who was this person? Then the penny dropped in the Egyptian's head,

"Of course, we are expecting an official United States aircraft from Cape Town later this evening carrying the Peace Envoy from The United Nations and his name was Sevilla! Could this be the same man and what the hell was he doing on a scheduled flight?" he thought to himself in a state of confusion.
With a man of this importance involved he (Airport Director) realized he had no other choice that to contact the President and inform him of the situation.
Down in deepest Angola the comprehensive search was well under way as aircraft of the Angolan Air Force flew a standard grid line pattern in their attempt to locate the wreckage of the stricken airliner. Hour upon hour the pilots and observers aboard the
C-130's and Antonov's scanned the dense forests below with binoculars.. but nothing, not the slightest sign of wreckage or broken trees ...nothing. There came a point of frustration when Abyara ordered that the search area be enlarged by at least one hundred miles in all directions in the possibility that the aircraft's position had been calculated incorrectly.
He himself, safely aboard the Gazelle

cruising at three thousand feet above the trees, was now running low of fuel so ordered the pilot to head back to Kuito for a top-up to then rejoin the search group in the enlarged zone..

Upon receiving the news of the missing Airbus and it's coveted passenger, Nasir Mohammed instantly felt a cold shiver running down his back all the way to his coxis as having not yet been informed of the problem with Air Force 6 could not understand why the Envoy would suddenly be on an International Airliner on a scheduled flight.

It would be another couple of hours of bewilderment before he would receive the somewhat 'delayed' call from President Khumab. Armed with this confirmed knowledge of the problem with the Gulfstream's engine and consequent change for Sevilla to a British Airways flight only served to enhance his deepening concern as to the possible repercussions from this disaster. Until the authorities had located and examined the wreckage to confirm exactly what had happened he had visions of the world's media going wild with speculation and casting aspersions in all directions. Having been the instigator of the acceptance of the Peace Plan Nasir Mohammed was now not a happy man

President O'Shea could not believe his ears when Khumab placed his call to the White House. There was a well engineered procedure to be followed by the crew in the event of an incident with one of the Presidential fleet of aircraft. This procedure had been breached enraging the American premier,

"*Why didn't the Gulfstream captain call in for assistance with an incident report?*" O'Shea asked.
" *You will have to ask him that yourself Mr President. All I know is that Señor Sevilla was insistent on authorising his team's transfer to a scheduled British flight. It was his decision to transfer. Your captain could not have stopped him!*" responded Khumab.
"*Oh very well Zubair but what is the latest on the search for the airliner?*"
"*No news to report at present. The Angolan Air Force are out in strength with at least fifty percent of their entire fleet. I too have requested our Air Force to join in with three*

C-130's I......"
Before Khumab could finish his sentence O'Shea interrupted,

" If there is no positive news within the day I will authorise my aircraft to join in. In the meanwhile I will make contact with Prime Minister Feldman in London and fill him in. Keep up the good work and let me know of any developments. Goodbye for now" and slammed the phone down with force.
"Martha get the Secretary of Defence here now!" O'Shea then shouted to his personal secretary who, on realising the President's concerned tone of voice, immediately dialled the Dept. of Defence.

Across the Atlantic in Whitehall Roger Feldman had already been primed of the situation in Angola by Sir Leonard of British Airways. Without hesitation the Royal Air Force had been contacted by M.O.D. (Ministry of Defence) to arrange to go and assist in the search.
The call from The White House came through to which Feldman showed no surprise. The conversation between him and President O'Shea took little time as they both agreed that more concrete information must

be ascertained before any further action or press release should be undertaken and it was further agreed that Feldman should act as the negotiator with those presently gathered in Cairo awaiting the Peace Agreement to arrive. Everything for the time being was to be kept on a friendly and low status basis until the cause of the aircraft loss was firmly established. This was to be no finger pointing, no implications and no innuendos made toward any faction or national, after all the crash when it is was found could well have been caused from a structural defect or pilot error. This had to be established at the earliest opportunity.

Feldman put through his call to Nasir Mohammed in Cairo who answered it in his private office. The conversation ended with them agreeing to wait until further developments had been established by either party who would then let the other know. In the meanwhile Mohammed would advice his guests to return to their homes and be prepared to return as and when the Peace Agreement eventually arrived in Cairo.

Those gathered round Mohammed's table looked each other in the eye and not a word was spoken but each could foresee dramatic events taking place in the region. Being as suspicious as they were each could suppose that the disappearing plane was no accident! At this stage all they could all do was to patiently wait and watch the internet.

Chapter Four

..."The Search Continues"

By sheer coincidence both the Royal Air

Force and the United States Air Force dispatched similar aircraft to the Gabon to join in the search for Speedbird 4674. The RAF Rivet Joint, Captained by Flight Lieutenant Kirk, had only just been delivered from the assembly line in California only days before, took-off from RAF Waddington in Lincolnshire amid storm clouds leaving four black trails of exhaust smoke leading into the low cloud. Not fifty miles to the south the American Rivet Joint had been readied at Mildenhall and was flight planned to depart at 1200 hrs.

Both these long range surveillance, spy planes were considered as they just had the range to reach Libreville Air Base in Gabon without requiring a mid-air refuel. These latest of aircraft carried a considerable array of electronic and optical sensors which would greatly assist the Gabon and Angolan Forces in the search. The flight time to Libreville had been calculated to be around eight hours.

One of the many observers aboard AN-72
A-GHYT ecstatically yelled out at the top of his voice,
" I have it! Down there in that clearing. I have it!"

Immediately the Captain closed the throttles and descended in a tight left turn toward the spot that the observer had indicated. Having attained a safe one hundred feet from the ground the Captain opened the throttles to maintain a comfortable speed of one hundred and seventy five kts giving all aboard a good opportunity to observe the wreckage for a confirmation.

Without doubt many aboard had spotted what appeared to be metallic wreckage strewn across the countryside, not a lot , but enough to call in Colonel Abyara in his Gazelle helicopter who could land and confirm the authenticity.

"Good looking Captain. I should be at your location in twenty minutes. Keep flying a holding pattern above the wreckage and guide us in" responded Abyara in his usual jolly voice.

The Gazelle Captain altered course to his south-East and proceeded on full power to locate the AN-72. In his eagerness to improve his personal standing Abyara could not hold back on informing base of the find. They in turn passed on the news to Cape Town who were so anxious to receive news.

It was in fact nearer twenty five minutes before the circling Antonov, which had been relaying video footage of the crash site back to Kuito Base which in turn was being surreptitiously intercepted by the Sky News satellite and shown to the world, came into the Gazelle's Captain's view,
"Gazelle to A-GHYT. I have you in sight. Fire a flare at the sighted wreckage" commanded the pilot.
Following the order a green trail emerged from the Antonov making it's way to the clearing on the ground.
As the dust kicked up by the rotor blades settled it allowed Colonel Abyara to step from the Gazelle and ran to the largest piece of wreckage heavily embedded into the soil. With close examination Abyara was able to identify the shape as a tailplane but on brushing away a few inches of dust and debris was then profoundly disappointed to read the marking written on the skin,
" ..dustries."
It was a private company aircraft! Abyara's jaw dropped like a brick in disappointment but he had to face the fact that this was **not** the missing Airbus. What they had found

might be of interest to Karma Industries, but not to British Airways or the waiting world. Back in the Gazelle he had the ignominy of informing Cape Town of the abortive find.

The search continued....

The hours passed, the relatives of the Airbus passengers who had now been made fully aware of the missing aircraft were clambering for news from British Airways at both Cairo and Cape Town Airports, world leaders waited for news and Douglas Myers , en-route to South Africa with the Technical Director of Airbus Industries, chewed his fingernails to the bone.

Still no sighting of any wreckage...

It had now been many, many, many hours since the last communication with the pilots of Speedbird 4674. Time for all the searching Angolan aircraft to receive another order from Colonel Abyara,
"Abyara to all search aircraft. Extend your search patterns out by another three hundred mile radius and if you have to cross into Zaire or Congo go ahead, I will clear it with the authorities."

Having seen the involvement of his country growing deeper by the hour especially with the anticipated arrival and consequent re-fuelling of the two Air Force spy planes, President Mombo decided to enlist the use of three of his Puma heavy helicopters to join in the search and to concentrate over the sea for any floating debris.
This now led to the involvement of aircraft from four countries in the search for the gigantic Airbus!
It took the senior Air Traffic Controller from Kinshasa to suggest contacting all other radar networks, both civilian and military, within Central Africa to verify the existence of any unknown radar traffic appearing on their scopes within the last fifteen or so hours. Not one controller could confirm any unaccounted for traffic..not one!

In the eyes of those in receipt of this information it could mean only one thing .. the aircraft must have crashed ..so why could no wreckage be located? The general conclusion amongst the powers that be was, that despite being miles and miles off course the Airbus must have ditched into water, but there was no lakes or water reserves big enough in the area, except the Atlantic Ocean! If it had gone down in the ocean ..what possible scenario could have developed allowing this to have happened?

The mystery of the disappearance of Speedbird 4674 deepened even further!

With barely enough fuel left in the tanks the large RAF four engined Rivet Joint spyplane touched down on runway 16R at Libreville's Leon M'ba International Airport which had the unusual aspect of running just a few metres from and parallel to the Atlantic. Once safely established on the taxiway and having completed his landing checks, Flight Lieutenant Kirk requested an immediate update of the search situation and a re-fuel before his secondary crew would commence engaging in an extended search on the sea to the north of Libreville.
No sooner had Kirk spooled down his
CFM-56 engines than the American Rivet Joint appeared in view on short finals to 16R. Her captain, having heard Kirk's ground instructions on the RT, similarly requested a re-fuel as he too would be considering a

search pattern over the sea but to the south. With absolutely no evidence whatsoever of where the Airbus might have crashed the American Captain wished to cover all possibilities however ludicrous they may seem hence his decision to hunt off the Congolese and Angolan coastlines leaving the RAF to the Cameroon, Equatorial Guinea and Nigerian coastal zones.
Surely with this amount of search power from the combined efforts of UK, USA, Gabon and Angola the elusive airliner would soon be discovered.

It was during his flight aboard the scheduled Speedbird 1345 en-route for Cape Town from London Heathrow that Douglas Myers was radioed the news that the Peace Envoy, Rodiguez Sevilla was aboard the doomed 380 and that the world media also were aware of this serving to focus the microscope of the press on the demise of the Airbus.
This did not sit well with the British Airways Operations Director who now realised that his inevitable press conference when he arrived in Cape Town would now be under extra scrutiny. He would have to expect immense personal pressure to come from The United Nations and world Governments

for an explanation as to why such a modern and highly advanced airliner flown by some of the most respected pilots in the business could just disappear. He had no answer but would have to come up with an acceptable and plausible explanation to satisfy the concerns of the relatives of the passengers, who he calculated would be congregating at Cape Town Airport.

"Cape Town Approach. This is Speedbird 1345 at FL 35 on heading 185 degrees and at two hundred miles, request GCA (Ground controlled approach)"

"Speedbird 1345 this is Cape Town. We have you on scope. Continue your approach on 185 and prepare to commence your descent to FL 20 in 10 for runway 19R" responded the Cape Town air traffic controller.

Within forty minutes the Operations Director's flight was safe on the tarmac of Cape Town's 19 runway and was about to taxy to Terminal 2 building to disembark it's blissfully innocent passengers excepting that of Douglas Myers and his personal secretary.

Still the vast search found no signs whatsoever of the remains of Speedbird 4674!

In Cairo, having bid farewell to all his Islamic colleagues as they departed back to their home towns in Syria, Palestine and Gaza, Nasir prepared for his own Middle-Eastern press conference hastily arranged to be delivered in the Mogamma Building in Tahrir Square. With no scripted agenda Mohammed took his seated position alongside the British Airways Station Manager in the centre of the stage, adjusted one or two of the multitude of microphones and opened the proceedings,
" Salaam... You are all aware that the British Airways flight carrying the historic Peace Agreement, escorted by the United Nations Envoy Rodriguez Sevilla, has met with a catastrophe. There are a considerable number of aircraft searching for the wreckage as I speak but as yet to no avail. At this stage it is generally assumed that structural damage was the primary cause of the disaster. British Airways here in Cairo have assured me that they will do everything possible to keep all the families and relatives fully informed and have further offered to accommodate those who want to be near the airport until the aircraft has been found. I will now take questions ."
Amongst the furore of waving hands and

shouting in their bid to get the first question in there appeared one familiar face who gained Mohammed's eye,
"Yes Yasmin. What is your question?"
"Yasmin of Cairo News. Mr President how many passengers were on-board?"
With a certain amount of embarrassment Mohammed passed this question to the BA Manager who took to his feet,
"Ladies and Gentlemen. Flight 4674 was a new Airbus 380-800 and the manifest showed that four hundred and twenty six passengers and fifteen crew were on-board. The captain was one of our most senior staff having five thousand flying hours under his belt. I can offer no explanation as to what might have happened" and sat down.
The questioning continued for another forty three minutes before Mohammed called time amid the shouting and flashing camera lights.

A similar press conference was well under-way in Cape Town International Airport with Douglas Myers taking the Praesidium. With no concrete news to impart to the information hungry relatives and press, except to confirm that The Peace Envoy and the historic Agreement were on-board BA

4674, Myers stumbled in his unprofessional but understandable delivery. What sympathy could he offer to the wailing and sometimes angry audience when he himself had no explanation to offer excepting that everything was being done to locate the wreckage.

The one and only really complicated question thrown at the struggling Director came from the middle of the audience, an unusually tall man dressed in a Dishdash stood up and yelled,
"Could the disappearance of your aircraft have anything to do with the Peace Agreement being carried on-board?"
Naturally, on hearing about Sevilla being amongst the passengers Myers thoughts had sided toward this possibility of a terroristic attack in an attempt to thwart the peace process but this suggestion could not be aired in public especially so early into the investigation. Myers replied,
"At this time I can see no connection. Next question please!"
The tall man left the room but not without the observance of the chief police officer stood near the entrance door. Using his shoulder radio the officer ordered one of his

plain clothed men to follow the suspect but to remain unobserved and report back every half hour.
The conference continued for several more minutes before the Airport Director called a halt.

By this time President Khumab appeared in the airport, no doubt in order to publicly sanctify his interest in the affair. He immediately made contact with his friend, the Airport Director for an update,
"Can we go to your office as I need to make a call?" requested the President.

"Of course come this way."
Having established the parties involved in the aerial search Khumab put a call through to his opposite number in Angola and following a lengthy introductory conversation Khumab finally came to the point,
"Have you any progress in finding any evidence of the disappearance of the BA Airbus?"
The reply was definite,
"None whatsoever Zubair. None of the search planes have found a single thing and none of our radars have shown any unplanned traces. The Americans and

British have sophisticated aircraft out over the sea but so far nothing. "
With dejection in both their voices the conversation ended.

"Search one. This is Leon M'ba control. Do you receive?"

"Leon M'ba this is Search One. Go ahead" replied Flight Lieutenant Smith as he initiated a starboard turn for the Rivet Joint.
"How is the search proceeding sir?"
"We have undertaken a north-south grid pattern between you and the Nigerian coast. Now on the third leg turning north once gain. So far nothing. No flotsam, nothing at all" replied the RAF captain.
The same was asked of 'Search Two' (the American Rivet Joint) who also responded with ..nothing.

The search continued into the evening dusk before all the captains headed back to their respective bases. They would resume at first light the following morning.
Not much sleep was achieved by many that night. Many in the airports were engaged in praying all night in the hope the something would be found the following day. So many

were anxious for answers.

Dawn broke over the African continent bringing a beautiful radiant red glow to the west coast all the way from Cameroon down to South Africa. The high cloud base and visibility presented the most perfect of conditions for all the aircraft to resume their search. With the urgency and mystery of the disappearance hitting a new depth the Premier's of Chad and Central African Republic offered what little they had at their disposal to assist in the search.
One Antonov AN-26 transporter and two Cessna Skymaster light surveillance aircraft were dispatched from N'Djamena International Airport to survey a central track through Chad whilst in Bangui in Central African Republic a single C-130 transporter took to the air.
Together with the joint effort from five other countries there was a total of nineteen aircraft in the air searching hard for BA 4674.
The world stood by waiting for some positive news.

Still nothing.

Unaware of the research going on in the

Intersat Satellite communications office in southern England to all, except those in the research department in Airbus Industries in Toulouse, France, Intersat was ploughing through their aircraft-satellite communication records for data that might help establish the last trajectory of BA 4674. Unbeknown, even to the senior and technical staff of British Airways, a small reactive computer had been installed into the 380 during manufacture which when interrogated on an hourly basis by the Intersat ring of satellites replied with a string of status data. The technical boys at Intersat studied the last responses from the 380 in the hope they might throw light on the gloomy situation. They did! Without doubt the BA 380 was still in the air nearly three and a half hours after take-off which was of no great surprise but it was the location that threw a spanner in the works!
The final signal received put the aircraft some four hundred miles off the coast of Gabon, in the Atlantic Ocean!
Immediately having been handed this information the CEO of Intersat made contact with Sir Leonard Foley of British Airways and informed him of this revelation. It was coincidentally that Foley had just

received written news from Rolls Royce of the confirmation of when the four on-board engine monitoring computers had ceased to transmit their engine parameter data via satellite to the Rolls Royce headquarters at Derby, England. This special technical feature was one of the unique selling points of all Rolls engines .. an hour by hour report of every active engine in service transmitted to the Derby Technical Department.

Having thanked all concerned for their information it dawned on Foley of the abnormality of the situation. He called into his Heathrow office the duty Senior Training Pilot to also examine the info and confirm or deny his own conclusion of the facts.

They both agreed ...it was impossible.

Intersat had put the Airbus 380 some four hundred miles off Gabon three and a half hours after take from Cape Town then the transmissions stopped indicating a possible crash, but the engine computers confirmed that the aircraft was still airbourne and transmitting engine data for another **four and a quarter hours!**

How could this be possible Foley asked in his ignorance.

The training captain gave some focussed thought to this highly unusual situation,

"There can only be one answer Sir Leonard, and one answer alone, the flight crew must have ***switched off*** *both their identification transponder and Intersat computer. Who was the captain of the flight sir?"* replied the rather worried Captain.

" Let me see, ah yes here we are Captain Brian Gunn."

"Brian, I know him well Sir Leonard. He was in for his six monthly flight check just a couple of weeks ago. He is one of our most senior pilots!"

" Did he seem any different from usual or perhaps worried?" asked Foley.

" He was fine Sir Leonard. I would trust him with my life, excuse the pun sir."

"But why would he have switched off those computers then?" asked Foley.

" I cannot answer that sir. On no account, absolutely no account would any airline skipper switch off his transponder, never unless,.........." pausing for a moment,

"Yes captain you were going to say.""Unless he wanted to ***disappear!!****"*

With this analogy in mind Foley had no choice that to impart this vital knowledge to none other than the Prime Minister himself and so arranged to meet Roger Feldman in

Downing St. at the earliest possible opportunity. On talking to Feldman's PPS this turned out to be within the hour.

Sir Leonard was led up the stairs and through to the PM's private office on the first floor where Roger Feldman was waiting sat behind his desk.

"Welcome Leonard come in and take a seat and tell me what info you have" greeted Feldman.
" I will come straight to the point Prime Minister. From confirmed information from Rolls Royce and Intersat and having talked with my Senior Training Captain an hour ago, it is my opinion ...... it is ***my*** *opinion that our flight, Speedbird 4674 that was carrying the United Nations Peace Envoy Señor Rodriguez Sevilla presumably with the 'Agreement', has either been hijacked or deliberately ditched by the plane's captain!"*

"What!!!!!!" yelled the Prime Minister as he stood up and thumped the desk,
"How the hell did you come up with that ?" he continued.
A prolonged discussion ensued with Feldman finally asking **the** question that sat on the

lips of many a politician but were too afraid to contemplate addressing ,

"Do you think it could have been shot down Leonard?"

Dead silence fell upon the office for what seemed an eternity before Sir Leonard offered his response,
"That cannot be ruled out Prime Minister ... but if that were the case there would be evidence of either a missile trace or unidentified fighter, surely?"
"Good point. What about a submarine then?" Feldman continued.
" Yes that would be untraceable but that would not explain why the aircraft was way out over the Atlantic and with no transponder activated?" replied Sir Leonard.
Quickly Feldman counter replied,
"Unless the Captain or First Officer were on a suicide mission and deliberately flew over the sea to be shot down."
"Jesus Christ! sir that is stretching it a bit isn't it?" the incensed CEO responded.
The meeting finally broke up with Feldman agreeing to order the Captains of both his

and the American Rivet Joints to extend their search further out into the Atlantic.
A further order, from the Ministry of Defence, was issued to all search aircraft to listen out for the tell-tale morse code signal that was designed to be transmitted from the aircraft's black box, that is in fact bright orange, for around thirty days following a crash.

With all those concerned in the location of BA 4674 fully updated, the search continued

....and continued.

Chapter Five

..."A Finger is Pointed"

The peace between Israel and Garza had now held for many days allowing both sides to attempt a re-build of their communities. Garzans in the main were still searching through the rubble of what used to be their houses, shops and Mosques in the vain hope of finding some survivors but more often than not, just turning up corpses of loved ones. The actual clearing of the mountains of debris pervading every street in the strip and re-building the community would take years to fully accomplish. But as the seven year blockade imposed by Israel had now been lifted the free access of goods and building materials from other countries and entry of humanitarian aid could rapidly ease the plight and serve to improve the living standards of those Garzans left following the massive Israeli bombardment of the last few months.

A national free and unfettered election had been hastily arranged for March 12th which would allow all Garzans to freely display their loyalty.. or so they were led to believe!
A period of peace, with enlarged territorial limits as agreed in the "Peace Agreement", was all that most had dreamed off. To be able to shop, send their children to school and conduct their lives without fear of a tank shell or aircraft missile bursting around them was a joy to behold.

Over the divide the average Israeli citizen was trying to come to terms with the reduction of their, or what they considered to be their, country. The boundary of the
'New Israel' would severely impose upon their population expansion plans and did not sit well with either the people or Government, however the thought of an overall and extended peace in the Middle-East would do much to sweeten the bitter taste.

They too had a debris clearance, albeit of a very limited amount, to achieve before normal life could resume to the towns and villages sat near to the old Garzan border.

Part of this clearance programme was the removal of the barbed wire fence erected many years previous, which ran the full inland length of the Garza Strip.

Way back since 1998 it had successfully kept under strict control any Garzans wanting to illegally infiltrate Israel. The only legal means of entry was by the two heavily guarded security gates. In a show of good faith toward the imminent signing and imposition of the 'Peace Agreement' Benayoun had ordered an immediate removal of the fence. The first of the Israeli military engineering units arrived at the central section on the morning of the 27th and began by digging at the foundations with their imported JCB diggers.

All was going well. Grab after grab the driver cutaway the soil until he suddenly stopped the engine of the digger, leapt from the cab and ran to view the huge hole that had just collapsed in front of the machine. Then with a guarded excitement in his voice shouted to his Commanding Officer stood some thirty

metres away,
"Sir, sir look what I have found. You must come and see this now sir!"
"What is it Private?" came the reply as Captain Cohen came rushing over.
"Look in there sir. It's a tunnel!"

Sure enough after a preliminary inspection of the deep hole Cohen agreed that there was a man-made tunnel which would have appeared to have collapsed under the stress of the repeated grabbing.
Without hesitation the Captain retrieved his mobile phone from his trouser pocket and dialled HQ requesting the presence of a Senior Officer and an armed engineering team to come and join him with immediate haste. In the meanwhile the JCB driver was ordered to clear the hole of some of the newly collapsed top soil.
Within the hour a full team of twenty fully armed soldiers from the Engineering Corps arrived in a truck with young Colonel Yaksic riding in the front cab,
"What is the panic Captain?" shouted Yaksic as he jumped from the cab.
"Well Sir, I can't be sure but I think we have just found a secret tunnel leading towards Netivot."

With a gay abandon the well decorated Colonel jumped into the hole and once back on his feet withdrew his torch from it's holster and shone it into the darkened abyss.

What befell him sent a shiver down his back. Sure enough it was a tunnel but one big enough the drive a car down!!! Fully lined with steel reinforcing and a floor of a mixture of compacted sand, rubble and concrete it was a professionally constructed underground highway capable of allowing jeeps and possible small armoured cars through.
The Colonel called for his team of engineers to join him as he gradually made his way down the tunnel in a westerly direction towards Garza. With their sub-machine guns at waist height and cocked for possible action the twenty strong unit wearily proceeded forwards with not a word passing between them. Maybe there could be an ambush. But what was the purpose of such an elaborate tunnel Yaksic kept asking himself.
Then out of the darkness as the torch beam trailed to his left Yaksic perceived another, but not quite so elaborate, tunnel. Then to his amazement when casting the torch around

the new tunnel there was yet another!
This was a truly extraordinary find ..a complete underground network of feeder tunnels from Garza leading into one main one that led towards Netivot... all this had been built in complete secrecy to enable a covert invasion of Israel and Israel had absolutely no knowledge of it's existence.
All that Yaksic could think of was that thank God they were now all at peace! There was however something else that intrigued the Colonel .. a door, an old steel blue door covered in rust,
"Shoot the lock Corporal" he ordered. A blast of bullets soon shattered the lock. Upon entry into the black hole Yaksic could not believe his eyes as he shone his torch; the small room of approximately twenty feet by thirty feet was filled to the ceiling with crate upon crate marked "**Grenades**", "**Rifles**", " **RPG**'s" but worse of all was a stack marked as "**Chemical**."
Not wishing to meddle with or even go near the "**Chemical**" crates for fear of picking up a contamination, Yaksic ordered one of the " **RPG**" crates to be smashed open. Inside was packed at least twenty brand new shoulder held Rocket Propelled Grenade launchers and grenades. All were still

wrapped in their original grey plastic paper. Unwrapping the top weapon Colonel Yaksic soon saw the manufactures plate displaying the serial number which confirmed that they were the latest DP-64 anti-tank variant from Russia. However the most revealing surprise came when he observed a folded piece of paper within the wrapping. It was an invoice! It was an invoice stating that the RPG's were supplied by the Russian Government directly to the Egyptian Brotherhood Government in Cairo! and the date: Just one week previous.... **after** the 'Peace Agreement' had been conceived and agreed to be signed!
At that point the Colonel had no choice than to order the "**RPG**" crates to be carried back to the truck and for a quantity of explosives to be brought back . In the meanwhile he waited in the room with two of his soldiers prepared to open fire on any Garzan or Hamas soldiers that might appear.
Soon enough five of his original men returned with a selection of H.E. (High explosive) which they proceeded to strategically arrange around the room. When all was ready and the full complement of soldiers well clear down the tunnel, Colonel Yaksic gave the order, *"Fire!"* and immediately there was a massive

explosion which brought the roof down closing off the back tunnel whilst filling the main tunnel with an obnoxious cloud of smoke and fumes. Job done.

Three thousand miles away off the west coast of Africa the search for BA 4674 continued unabated. Even a Squadron of C-130's from the Nigerian Air Force had now joined in the air search whilst the Naval Directorate had ordered a selection of their Luerssen and Combattante Patrol boats equipped with underwater sonar detectors, to put to sea and listen out intently in the hope of picking up the low frequency but limited range Black Box signals.
The British Navy had also been ordered to divert HMS Argyll, a Type 23 Frigate which happened to be en-route to Gibraltar to participate in a NATO exercise, down into Nigerian waters and utilise her exceptionally sensitive sonar and underwater radar technology.
The search had now become massive.....
but still no positive news.

The Diplomatic fraternity around the globe were starting to show signs of unease as the press had no hesitation in spreading all sorts

of rumours and innuendos as to what happened to the Airbus and who or what might had been responsible.
The search was now into it's fourth day and with absolutely no sign whatsoever of any wreckage or more importantly no logical explanation of why or how! The interest of the global press grew more intense as each day led into another.

By special request Colonel Yaksic had been permitted an audience with the full Israeli Inner-Council along with his direct superior Officer Major-General Moshe Rosenburg. They had driven from their barracks and entered the impressive Knesset Parliament Building at Giv'at Ram in Jerusalem escorted by a small detachment of four soldiers. Together they all marched up the main steps through various imposing corridors to the Council's personal Chamber where they were meet by the Diplomatic Guard.
"The Council are waiting for you Sir" spoke the Guard as he opened the door.
This was the first time Yaksic had had the privilege of viewing the inner sanctum of his Government and was immediately impressed by it's splendour and huge mahogany circular conference table around which was sat ten

individuals.
"Good Morning General Rosenburg and of course Colonel Yaksic. To what do we owe this request for an audience? I understand you consider it to be of importance?" asked Prime Minister Benayoun.
"It is Prime Minister, it is" replied the General who promptly ordered the soldiers to place the heavy crate on the beautifully polished table.
"This sir was found by my colleague yesterday in a hitherto undiscovered network of secret tunnels emanating from Garza.. Crates and crates of these RPG's and much more was discovered. All, apart from this crate have now been destroyed and ......"
One of the Council then interrupted,

"Is this all you wanted us to gather here for General?"
"No sir, this was the reason!" and handed the Councillor the invoice found in the RPG wrapping.
Silence fell for a while.
"What is it ?" asked Benayoun.
"It's just an invoice Prime Minister from Russia to the Brotherhood in Cairo for a large consignment of ......"
"It's the date sir, the date that is important,

read out the date sir!" bellowed the impatient General Rosenburg.
"Oh my God!" shouted out the elderly Councillor, *" It's just for a few days ago!!"*
To push his point fully home Rosenburg proceeded to advise the Council that the crate marked '**RPG**' so innocently resting on the table were the latest technology from the Russian arsenal,

"So the question we should be asking ourselves is why are these here and when were they going to be used but more, much more importantly are the Brotherhood now tied together with Hamas?" Rosenburg addressed to the Council.
Dead silence as the Council of ten began to take in the implication of what the General had just said.
The silence continued until Benayoun spoke in a soft, worrying voice,
"Take a seat General and you too Colonel and send the men out please."
For the next hour the debate was thrown from one side to the other, tempers flew and opinions of all scenarios were considered but after a couple of hours a general conclusion was reached which had to be accepted by the complete Council: Mohammed of the

Egyptian Brotherhood had formed an alliance with Ahmad Habib of Hamas and were planning to invade Israel by gaining entry through the underground tunnels. In their candid view there could be no other conclusion to reach! But what to do now? To openly accuse Mohammed now could be fatal for the eventual signing of the Treaty if their conclusion was wrong, to do nothing again might prove fatal if an attack was imminent, to strike at Hamas now would bring world condemnation upon the name of Israel and bring the '**Peace Treaty**' to a sudden halt. Their hands were tied and the air of frustration could be felt around the room.
It took a statement from the Prime Minister to conclude the meeting,
"Gentlemen having listened to all your views we are certainly between a rock and a hard place. We have no choice than to very quietly prepare for an invasion. No outward sign of our preparation must be visible to the outside world. General you will arrange a covert, a very covert search for anymore tunnels and then you will construct a defence profile at the head of each one. Meanwhile, gentlemen I will contact President O'Shea and confidentially fill him in. Do you all agree?"

A show of nine hands confirmed the arrangement.

Still the search in the Atlantic and over the forests of central Africa continued but to no avail.
Press conference after press conference took the media stage in Cape Town, London and even Cairo. Answers were sought but none could be given!

What had happened to BA4674?

The situation had now become so bizarre and inexplicable that America altered the trajectory of two of it's spy satellites to fly an orbit taking in the mid Atlantic in the hope they might be able to locate items of floating wreckage.

President O'Shea was taking a well earned ten minute siesta in his private study away from his busy schedule when he was awakened by his secretary,
"Sorry to disturb you Mr President but you have an incoming call of importance from Prime Minister Benayoun of Israel" and left the room.

"Jesus Christ! Jacob this is very serious indeed. I want you to fax me a copy of this invoice and I will contact you again tomorrow. Will you do that please?" O'Shea requested having understood the situation.

Having jumped to his feet O'Shea called back his secretary to cancel the remaining appointments of that day and call an emergency meeting of the Joint Chiefs of Staff in the Oval Room for 6pm.
The pacing up and down of the study floor began to create a ploughed rut in the sumptuous dark blue carpet but O'Shea just could not figure out what the best course of action should be. The effort over the past months that he and his colleagues as well those in the UK and the Middle-East had expelled in negotiating the
'**Peace Agreement**' seemed to have now been in vane if Hamas and the Brotherhood were planning to invade during the forthcoming period of peace.

But what to do now?

5.55pm was clearly displayed on O'Shea's Omega wristwatch as he walked through the Oval Room door. The room was full of military uniforms, Navy, Air Force, Army ,

Coast Guard and Reserves with gold braid and decorations glinting in the evening sunshine as it pierced through the vast array of south facing windows. The room stood to attention,

" Gentleman good evening. I have called you here at such short notice. We might have a problem ..a big one and I want your professional input" continued the President.

The fax was produced from inside O'Shea's inside pocket and passed around the room,

"Opinions please" asked the President.

With the experience that all the Chiefs of Staff held at their combined disposal the eventual recommendation as what to do was completely unanimous. Admiral Strickland took the lead and ventured their joint accessment,

*"Invade Egypt Mr President!. We have to send a message to the whole Islamic community that the '**Peace Agreement**' is to stand."*

Then the Chief of the Air Force spoke out,

"Sir, could I put forward the theory that it was the Brotherhood that took out the British flight and Air Force 6 to destroy the agreement?"

Once again a silence descended on the room.

The Chief of the Navy spoke,
"Why do that, it is only a book that could be re-written."
The Air Force General answered,
"Because The Brotherhood could claim that the 'agreement' was shot down by us or the British which would give them credence to invade Israel!"
The irate President O'Shea raised his hands in the air to focus the room's attention, *"Gentlemen, we will wait a period of one month from today to allow the missing British aircraft to be found and it's cause of destruction firmly established. It will also give Hamas time to show their hand as to their intentions. Then I will decide on our final action, meanwhile I want a plan of the invasion of Egypt to be secretly and Gentlemen I do mean under the strictest of confidentiality, drawn up and brought before me for approval should we embark on this course of action. That will be all."*
The room emptied.
Later that day O'Shea informed both Benayoun and Prime Minister Feldman of this decision.

The pressure for news was building in Cairo.

Every day Terminal 2 at Cairo International became embedded with bereft relatives and friends of the missing passengers getting more anxious and unruly by the day. Without fail the British Airways Station Manager held a daily public conference in the terminal at 3pm. Each day the mood of the audience became more violent to the point that on day nine several members of the public broke through the security cordon in front of the stage and physically assaulted the Manager.

Media coverage of this behaviour fed down to Cape Town where a similar situation, although not so violent, action ensued when Douglas Myers appeared for his conference the following day.

Still the search for the missing flight continued .. no news or sighting!

Chapter Six

..."Decision Time"

It had now been almost a month since the disappearance of Speedbird 4674 and despite the enormous resources thrown into the

extensive search by several countries as well as many private organisations nothing, absolutely nothing had been found of the Airbus.
Described as the aviation mystery of all time there could be no corner of the globe where hypothesises to explain the disappearance were not being formulated.
The internet was full of chatter, diagrams and personal explanations. Despite the avalanche of concern shown for the passengers and their relatives very little had been displayed for the whereabouts of the
'**Peace Agreement**' or it's Envoy.... except , of course, by those officials who had been engaged in it's construction. Those officials were now becoming uncomfortable and many, including President O'Shea, Prime Minister Feldman, President Akbari, Robert Kuok and Prime Minister Benayoun, were calling for a new agreement to be drawn up. Nasir Mohammed of the Brotherhood and the other Islamic leaders had not yet shown the same enthusiasm which only led to further speculation as to why!
This lack of interest made the normally calm, resolved O'Shea very, very nervous.
Prime Minister Feldman had held covert meetings with MI6 who had agreed to

dispatch their best operative, Group Captain Dick Barton, out to Cairo and use and abuse his Egyptian contacts from the past to infiltrate the Brotherhood inner circle and gain intelligence.
Having suffered a degree of pressure from 'M' whilst he was serving at his post in MOD (Ministry of Defence) in London as an overseas attaché, Barton, an ex-RAF Harrier fighter pilot had been seduced into the shady world of spying and espionage due to his command of the Egyptian language and confidential behaviour which he used to great effect during his 'Go between' position with the Brotherhood when the negotiating the British terms of the '**Peace Agreement.**'
Barton readied himself for the scheduled British Airways flight to Cairo departing the following day from London's Heathrow Airport.
He found it somewhat compelling as he coincidentally passed a press conference about the missing BA flight being given in Terminal 5, as he checked-in for his BA 3214 flight to Cairo but chose to ignore the spectacle and proceeded directly to the gate at B17.

Exactly the opposite opinion and ideas to those being pro founded in Washington, were being discussed in the burning heat of Cairo. Nasir Mohammed had gathered together his close circle of senior officials in a private room in the Mogamma to consider the options open to them.

All, except Mohammed himself, were of one accord in their thinking: It was accepted by the Council of ten that the CIA had deliberately staged the failure of the AF6 Gulfstream's engine to enable the
'**Peace Agreement**' to be legitimately carried aboard a scheduled flight to Cairo which had then been arranged to 'disappear' giving the United States a bona-fide reason to suspect a Middle-Eastern country's involvement. This could then be used to pass a United Nations mandate for a full scale attack on the Middle-East with the backing of the West and Russia.
This thought brought terror to them all, but how could they either protect themselves or should they strike first with a series of terroristic atrocities on soft western targets.
Mohammed, having been the instigator of the
'**Peace Agreement**' in the first place

could not come to grips with the possibility of them striking first which would undoubtedly scupper any form of peace in the region for decades to come. Then on the other hand if they did nothing and an attack was made by the United States there would be no peace anyway especially if Israel was in on the attack!
Without knowing it Mohammed was in exactly the same position as President O'Shea ...between a rock and a hard place!

All things considered the Council decided to wait and do nothing ..for the time being!

The Group Captain's flight landed on time in the warm evening at Cairo International. Having cleared customs he briskly walked outside the main entrance and hailed a yellow coloured taxi,
"Salaam. Good evening sir. Where to please?" asked the driver.
"King Tut Hostal in Talaat Harb St please" replied Barton in his best Egyptian.
The twenty five kilometre drive down the dual carriageway of El-Orouba and Ramses streets and then into Talaat Harb took all of one and a half hours in the horrendous traffic.

During his previous negotiations with the Brotherhood Council, of a few months earlier, the British Officer needed to both impress his Egyptian colleagues as well as having the availability of conference rooms on tap so he stayed at the famous Four Seasons Hotel. With it's dramatic views across the Nile and sumptuous interior furnishings it provided extreme comfort for him during his time in Cario, however, on this visit he was ordered to play a much more covert game. For that reason he had booked a very down market and inconspicuous establishment occupying the eighth floor of No.5 Talaat Harb St .
Not being familiar with the entrance or interior décor of the King Tut, Barton was somewhat taken aback by the ultra low standard it had to offer. To the average western tourist it would have been classed as a tip, more akin to a slum really, but then what could he have expected for three pounds sterling a night which included a light breakfast!
It would serve it's purpose though as MI6 agent Barton might well need to disappear into the woodwork during his mission. Fully realising the sensitivity of the political

situation and not knowing which way the Brotherhood's wind was blowing he felt it advisable to be able to 'blend in' and perhaps disappear off the Brotherhood's radar should the need arise.
Once settled in the tiny room number 8 his first action after unpacking his meagre belongings was to pop down to the street and purchase a galabeya robe. To be taken as an Egyptian you first have to dress like an Egyptian. Together with his command of the language and his well manicured dark tanned complexion the MI6 operative could easily be accepted as one of the community should the need arise.

Still the search for Speedbird 4674 continued. Still nothing!

Aviation analyst's, commercial pilots, airline executives, journalists and broadcasters alike were daily submitting their theory's throughout the global media machine as to their explanation for the disappearance of 4674, but none could hold the light of credibility... but there had to be an explanation!

On receiving the various broadcasts on their

internet devices such as smart phones and ipads, the average Muslim who formed the backbone of the various fundamentalist factions throughout the Middle-East were gradually becoming suspicious and weary of the careless and to their minds discriminating suppositions being aired, tension was beginning to build once again particularly in Syria where the discontent of the so called militants began to spill across into the Golan Heights. Clashes between these militants and Israeli soldiers began to be reported more and more in the press as the eventual return of their land became more and more of a priority whilst escaping the clutches of President Gorani.
Immense public pressure was being brought to bear on Benayoun to control the situation as was the military strategist's pressure to invade Gaza was building as well.

In the corridors of power in Whitehall, London, the diplomatic machine, fronted by The Prime Minister and fully backed by the Opposition in the House of Commons, in order to placate all parties had put forward the agenda of the drawing up of another '**Peace Agreement**' to be re-signed by all

those on the lost agreement with all possible haste.
The majority of the assignees agreed with this plan but it was the American Senate , The Brotherhood Council and Israeli Council who showed reluctance to do so until the cause of the disappearance of flight 4674 had been firmly and truthfully established. This delay served only to heighten the tension.
It was now time, thought Prime Minister Feldman to throw substantially more resources into the search for the missing aircraft. Only when it was found and the Black Box analysed could the tension be lowered and a new agreement drawn up.
To this effect both the General Staff of the Royal Navy and Royal Air Force were commanded to immediately throw all possible effort into West Africa as a matter of the utmost priority.

Orders were sent from the Admiralty to vessels operating in the Mediterranean theatre on current assignments:
HMS Talent, a nuclear class submarine,
HMS Ocean, an amphibious Assault ship with fifteen Apache helicopters on-board and HMS Echo, a specialist survey vessel.
The RAF dispatched three giant C-17

transport, two C-130J transport and two Voyager re-fuellers from RAF Brize Norton in Oxfordshire and a E-3D Sentry (Hawkeye Command and Control) from RAF Waddington in Linclonshire.
The missing aircraft just had to be found.
With cooperation sought from the technical division of British Airways and Airbus Industries the overall command centre at RAF Waddington had calculated the maximum range that the Airbus 380-800 with a similar load as Speedbird 4674 to be an incredible eight thousand four hundred miles from Cape Town.
This enlarged the possible search circle to include as far as Rio de Janeiro, London and Mumbai, in other words the whole Atlantic Ocean, the whole African Continent and Arabian gulf to the Indian Ocean!
However, as most of the land is covered by so many different radars, none of which had admitted to having observed any unknown traces on their scopes, the Commanding Officer at Waddington had ruled out a land search. His area of greatest interest was the expanse of the mighty Atlantic. Any land search around where the aircraft has lost contact was being thoroughly searched by local Air Forces in any event.

The days turned into weeks as the greatest search in aviation history continued over the dark waters of the Atlantic. It had been nearly two months since the aircraft disappeared. Many items of flotsam and jetsam were picked up on the sensitive radars on-board the Rivet Joint aircraft but all turned out to be wooden crates, fishing nets and various other cargoes including an enormous container, discharged by commercial shipping at some time in the past ..but nothing that could be construed as aircraft wreckage ..nothing, absolutely nothing.

President O'Shea, having kept his eye on the ball from a daily intelligence report from his Chief's of Staff was coming up to his decision point of one month and called a staff meeting in the Oval Room.

No new information was forthcoming from any of those present except to report that the clashes in the Israel region of the Golan Heights was escalating and massive troop movements had been detected in Gaza by U2 spyplanes.

Following a subdued discourse the President stood up,
"Gentlemen I do not have enough as yet to order you to go to war. We must give peace as much chance as possible but by God we are close! I will liaise with the British Intelligence for an update. We will meet here again in two weeks. Gooday."

Barton had made inroads with the Brotherhood having been granted several meetings with a range of familiar officials of a lower status. Mohammed was aware of Barton's presence in the Mugamma but just could not fully appreciate as to the reason for him being in Cairo. He was nevertheless intrigued enough to summon Barton for a private discourse.
The day started well for the Group Captain as he confidently strode through Talaat Square in the morning sunshine, making his way to the Mugamma. The meeting with Nasir was for ten thirty giving him plenty of time to cross the heavily congested Tahrir Square and enter the huge Government Building.
Barton felt his fawn suit and open shirt to be appropriate for this occasion.
"Salaam, good morning Group Captain.

Come and take a seat " greeted the tall leader of the Brotherhood.
"Salaam Mr President. Good to see you again" holding out his hand in friendship.
Not one for protocol and idle talk Mohammed came straight to the point,
" I had been informed that you were in Cairo and I am curious to know why Group Captain?"
A lump developed in Barton's throat not expecting quite such a direct approach from his colleague,
"My Government has sent me as the 'Go between' to act as the conduit between us in view of the demise of the "Peace Agreement". Nothing more" responded Barton .
But why you. I have your British Ambassador for that !"
"True but he is not well versed in military matters or searching for missing aircraft, whereas I am" the nervous Barton replied.

"Ah, yes I see that. Very well. What is the latest news for the search then?" Mohammed asked.
"We have many planes and ships covering half the Atlantic Ocean at present so we are expecting news soon Mr President" Barton replied hoping that this explanation should

satisfy Mohammed's curiosity for the time being. It did. The meeting was over and Barton departed promising to keep Mohammed informed of progress.

Walking passed one of the offices his attention was suddenly drawn to a familiar voice, that of Abdul Karim whom Barton knew to be an important man in the Egyptian organisation. Shielding against the wall Barton listened carefully at the door. His linguistic ability now came in handy. The conversation was mundane until the words 'Entry in Gaza tunnels'.. registered,

"Can I help you?" suddenly emerged from Barton's rear.

"*Er, er no just felling a bit feint from the heat and needed a little rest"* he quickly replied.

"Would you like some water?"

"No I'm feeling a little better now, thank you" and walked on towards the stairs.

Back at the King Tut, Barton thought and thought about the phrase he overheard., 'Entry in Garza tunnels.'

This could be of significance to MI6 so he made a mobile call to London.

Barton was correct. The powers in MI6, now

fully briefed on the Israeli situation and the deadlines set by President O'Shea, sat up in horror when advised of Barton's revelations. The pieces of the political jigsaw were beginning to fit into place.
O'Shea was kept informed of this crucial snippet of information. Now he was on edge and upon engaging this information with his CIA Director ....the time had come for positive action, was their joint conclusion. A war meeting of the Chief's of Staff was immediately convened.
The meeting lasted for several hours and only when a unanimous vote was obtained could war be declared. The reservations forwarded by The Chief of Coastguards had to be talked through and considered before a final decision could be issued. In the end The Chief's point of circumstantial evidence was crushed and he too raised his hand to action.
After further discussion as to what action should be taken it was agreed that it should take the form of a bombing raid upon the Brotherhood Government building, the Mugamma, as well as the three top airfields housing the Mig and F-16 fighter jets. The raid was to take place within the week with the flight planning and logistics to be undertaken entirely by the Air Force but to

be finally authorised by the President himself. Prime Minister Benayoun was to be kept fully informed especially as to the exact date and time of the attack and would be advised to be primed and ready for any reprisal attack from Hamas.

Still no news for the search of the missing A380!

As the days passed the preparations for the departure of the bombers and their crews from Whiteman Air Base in Missouri became complete and awaited their departure clearance from the White House.
The Chief of Coastguards slept little over these last few days fearing that his change of heart, for the concern of a first strike, was mistaken. Falling to his better conscience he eventually made tracks to the President's Office for a private one to one with O'Shea.
"What! a change of heart.. at this stage Admiral..Why??" shouted the normally docile O'Shea.
"I just feel we may live to regret a first strike without first giving Mohammed the opportunity of an explanation first, Mr President."

Gently caressing his chin with the thumb and index finger of his right hand, President O'Shea took a little time to contemplate his Chief's concerns whilst viewing the magnificent lawns through the bullet proof bay window,
"You're right of course Admiral. I will get our Ambassador in Cairo to approach Mohammed ASAP and see what he has to say" responded O'Shea *"but the plan of actions stands although with a possible delay should Mohammed's explanation be unacceptable."*
"Thank you Mr President I do feel that the people of America will thank you for that when all of this becomes public," the General related as he came to the salute before leaving the room.

Before Ambassador Preston was to be given acceptance to enter the room, Nasil Mohammed, having smelt a rat by this speedy and insistent request for an audience, had invited the British Group Captain to be present. From their previous business experience Barton had gained Mohammed's trust, whereas all Americans, especially those representing the Republicans, were to be given a wide berth. Something of a political bombshell was about to be dropped in his lap, so sensed Mohammed and he wanted a trusted colleague of both sides to be a witness to this possibility.

"*Well Salaam and good morning to you Mr. President*" spoke the ever confident and experienced Preston as he boldly entered the room.

"And to you Ambassador" replied Mohammed, *"You know Group Captain Barton. I asked for him to be here to assist in whatever matter you have come to speak to me about. You have any objection to that?"* as he pointed to the figure partially hidden by the enormous papyrus plant strategically placed near the window.

Preston was instantly cemented to the spot with surprise as he had requested a private audience with the Leader of the Brotherhood.

But what choice had he been given,

"No of course not!" Not being aware that Barton worked for MI6 having only briefly been introduced as an attaché in the past, *"How are you Group Captain? .....I will come straight to the point sir. I have been asked by my President to ask you if you have recently been supplying arms to Hamas?"* Preston asked as sweat became

clearly visible as it trickled down from his forehead.
Mohammed had not anticipated this question and thought quickly as he sat down before delivering what he thought to be a diplomatic reply,
"Of course Mr Ambassador, but what do you consider to be recent?"
*"Since the inception of the '**Peace Agreement**' sir"* replied Preston.
A few seconds passed,
"Now I see. This has to do with the missing aircraft a.........."
Preston interrupted,
"That must not be seen as the reason sir!"
Time for Barton to voice his observation,
"Gentlemen, Mr Ambassador you obviously had reason to convene this meeting. Would you oblige us."
"So British, Group Captain no messing about. Very well. We are in possession of an invoice to you (looking directly at the Brotherhood Leader) from Russia for a consignment of arms that were found in a tunnel in Israel, sir, the date of which was just a few days ago. Can you explain that Mr President?"
Mohammed's head dropped as he turned and walked to the window for a few seconds to

contemplate his response.
On turning back to face his inquisitor and started to speak, the previous politeness of the room's atmosphere visibly changed,
" I can now see the reasoning behind your visit Mr. Preston and I take great exception to it Sir! Great exception indeed! You are accusing the Brotherhood of downing the British aircraft to scupper the Agreement pending an attack on Israel from Hamas. My answer will be to no avail to O'Shea I fear. I bid you farewell Mr Preston."
The embarrassed Preston hurriedly left the room to make his report directly to President O'Shea impatiently waiting in his private quarters in the White House.
The somewhat surprised Barton faced an anxious Mohammed,
" Is that true Sir?"
"Group Captain, as a military man you well know that you should be prepared for your enemy to act in a way that may not be as he had stated. Hamas have always been so suspicious of the Americans and took preventative action in the event of the Agreement being a 'white elephant' or 'distraction'."
"So you did supply the weapons then!" commented Barton.

"What do you think Group Captain?" came the reply with a hint of a smile creeping across his face.

The non-committal response from Cairo angered O'Shea to the point of calling in his Chief's of Staff once more, only this time to tell them of war ..not ask for their approval!

The decision was made.

Chapter Seven

..."The Spirit's Fly High and Far"

Colonel Piratin proudly and confidently walked into the briefing room conveniently located one hundred feet below ground in a complex array of corridors to which the only exit/entry was by way a lift which conveyed it's occupants from ground level down to the massive nuclear bomb proof door to the underground system. The seven officers present immediately stood to attention.

"Sit down Gentlemen please" uttered the six foot two Texan as he took the stage behind the lectern.

"Sorry for the cloak and dagger briefing guys but we have all been selected for a 'black ops ' in the Middle-East which is of the highest classification. From this point on none of us is to communicate with anyone, especially family, about this operation. Do you all understand?"

To a man the response was "*Yes sir.*"

The Colonel continued,

"Our target is central Cairo and three surrounding airfields. Ordnance will be Mk 84's 2000 pounders, sixteen on each of the four aircraft. Major's Andersen, Fox and Derrick plus myself will skipper Spirit of New York, Indiana, Texas and Florida.

ETD 0700hrs tomorrow for Fairford, UK for en-route attack profile configuration. Go study the route and your targets in these orders. Be at final dispersal briefing 0630hrs. Good day Gentlemen." Piratin handed out the seven sealed A4 folders, each marked

"Top Secret"

in red, diagonally written across the front cover.
None of the eight pilots slept well that night. The thought of these awesome stealth bombers being ordered into live action was a serious business. As professional as they all were, for the States to employ such 21st century technology had to indicate the near proximity of an all out war!
Orders are orders, especially from such a great height, and to a man they would not question them. There was no hesitation shown by any of the experienced flight crew in accepting their task. They would do it and do it well. Years and years of training had led to this point in their careers. They had been selected over the other sixteen B-2A Spirit crews and pride and honour would prevail.
Having only been formed around ten years previously the elite 13th Bomb squadron, attached to the 509 Operations Group, was based at Whiteman Air Force Base in

Missouri and consisted of only twenty aircraft ..the mighty B-2A Spirit Stealth bomber. This futuristic 'flying wing' was unique in it's design in that it is practically invisible to radar. It's uncanny shape, integrated weapons bay and unique surface paint manifested the smallest of radar signatures on enemy scopes, rendering this huge machine undetectable.

With the final brief complete all eight Commissioned Officers walked to their 'Spirit's of the Sky' innocently waiting on the dispersal pad outside Hanger S1.

Northrop Grumman **B-2A Spirit** Stealth bomber

Piratin and his co-pilot Major Grey climbed aboard and strapped themselves into the tiny cockpit of 'Spirit of New York' in preparation for the nine and a half hour flight to the United Kingdom.
"Glad I had that hearty breakfast Colonel. This is a long trip" spoke out Grey as she clipped on her facemask.
"Me too Major. Brought some sandwiches though for half way!" responded Piratin.
Checks complete Piratin checked in with the other three for a comms link..all good,
" Death Squadron to control ready for start-up" the Colonel communicated to the tower.
"Death Squadron. All are clear go ahead sir."
As Piratin depressed the auto start sequence toggle, one by one the almighty General Electric F118's fired into life. Within seconds the characteristic 118 idling whistle from sixteen engines could clearly be discerned over the din of other air traffic on the airfield. Temperatures, pressures and flight plan all checked and verified,
"Death 1 to control ready to taxy" called Piratin.
"Cleared to taxy to runway 09L. Wind 010 degrees 5 kts."
"09L, 010 Death 1."

The engine note changed to a deep growl as Piratin allowed Grey to ease the throttles forward a little encouraging the huge aircraft to move forward towards the runway. 'Indiana', 'Texas' and 'Florida' followed close behind.

Soon all four aircraft were sat on the end of the runway in a box formation,

"*Death squadron to control. Ready for take-off*" called Piratin.

"*Whiteman Tower to Death Squadron I have a special relayed call for you .... Gentlemen this is President O'Shea. Just wanted to wish you all good luck. This is a very important and sensitive mission. Hit your targets hard. Safe flight......... Death Squadron you are now cleared for take-off*" completed the controller.

No sooner had the controller authorised the take-off, when the elated Colonel Piratin plunged his four throttles fully forward to the stops..the engine note turned to an apocalyptic roar as the full one hundred thousand pounds of thrust exited the exhaust nozzles.

"*V1, rotate, V2*" issued Piratin as the speed rapidly built to the take-off speed of one hundred and forty five knots.

Now Andersen's 'Indiana' began to roll. No

sooner than it got airbourne off set 'Texas' and then 'Florida.' Within minutes all four of the imposing machines were safely airbourne, undercarriage stowed, flaperons at zero degrees and formatting on Piratin's 'New York' on a climbing heading of 095 degrees.
"Death 1 established in climb. Switching to Mid-State radar control on 126.95" Piratin advised Whiteman Tower.
"Acknowledged sir. Good luck Colonel."
So the long flight to RAF Fairford in Gloucestershire, England continued.

Meanwhile half-way across the world over the Eastern Atlantic Ocean the Rivet Joints and assisting aircraft and Naval ships were still observing their search patterns but any hope of finding the missing A380 was fading extremely fast, as one airline executive said at his conference in Cape Town, *"it's like trying to find a particular grain of sand in the Sahara Desert!"*
Weeks had now passed since it's disappearance. The world's media was now beginning to drop the story from their front pages and replacing it with more current events .

Several leaders, including Benayoun, Mohammed, Sawali, Akbari but most forcefully Robert Kuok of the United Nations were calling for a new '**Peace Agreement**' to be drawn up and signed as a matter of urgency. Others were more cautious and wanted a conclusion to the mysterious disappearance of BA 4674 first.

Once again tension was mounting in political circles.

"Fairford Tower this is Death Squadron approaching from the west on a heading of 165 degree at flight level 25. Request permission to enter circuit" requested the tired Major Grey.

"*Death Squadron. We have you. Cleared to land on runway 09R. Wind 025 10 kts.*"

The lights of the huge ten thousand foot runway became visible through the cockpit glass of Death 1. Piratin could easily see the early morning mist gently rising from the damp airfield grass.

"*Gear and full flaperon Major*" called the Colonel as he gradually eased the throttles back to thirty five percent to attain the approach speed of one hundred and eighty five knots.

Down 'New York' came over the Gloucestershire fields on it's long final approach path into RAF Fairford. Known by it's prefix as RAF (Royal Air Force) Fairford is actually an American base.
A text book flare and landing was achieved smack on the white threshold as Piratin pulled the throttles back to fully idle and applied the brakes. As soon as 'New York' was fully on the taxy way, Death 2 touched down shortly followed by Death 3 and 4.
As the low sun rose all four aircraft were lined up on the dispersal pad outside the specially air-conditioned hangers on the western end of the airfield.
The reception committee for the arrival of their special visitors consisted of the Station Commander, Lieutenant General Abe Samsonite, his deputy and the Weapons Director.
"Welcome to Fairford Colonel on this epic mission" greeted Samsonite as Piratin stepped onto the concrete.
Coming to the salute with their right hands held parallel to the ground over their right eye, Piratin and Grey acknowledged their greeting,
"Good morning Sir" spoke Piratin.
"I have arranged for you and your crews to

be billeted in the mess for a few hours rest Colonel and your aircraft will be re-fuelled and fully armed for your 1800hrs departure to Egypt" advised General Samsonite who then showed the eight officers to the waiting mini-bus.

With the area clear of personnel out came the multitude of bomb trailers from the lower confines of the voluminous hangers. Four to each Spirit with each carrying four ominous dark grey 2000 lb bombs each capable of inflicting massive damage. Very carefully each was winched up and loaded into the aircraft's internal rotary bomb rack until all sixteen were firmly installed into each aircraft.

Fully fuelled together with all maintenance checks completed the four impressive B-2A Spirits sat there in readiness to go to war.

Time ticked by as Colonel Piratin, awarded the Medal of Honour for his earlier exploits over Iraq in the Rockwell B1, slept soundly.

From the various amounts of intel forwarded to him by MI6 Barton, known within the Ministry for his sixth sense and uncanny perception, was feeling somewhat uneasy when reading between the lines. The last two or three e-mails he received did not quite

carry the usual intenseness of meaning as previous ones did. Something was not being told to him but then he suspected there was a hidden message within the text.
Acting on pure impulse alone he made tracks to visit The Mogamma in Tahrir Square for the third time in just as many days. Would Mohammed see him without an appointment ..fate would soon tell.
Fate was not being kind that day as Mohammed was visiting a Mosque somewhere in the North of Cairo or so Barton was advised by one of the office staff. Barton detected a bad karma encompassing his very body whilst in the huge building so made haste to exit into the hustle and bustle in the street outside. Then as he reached the far side of the road a Mercedes he recognised passed him by .. it was Mohammed's. Frantically waiving to attract the drivers attention the Group captain tripped and fell to the ground causing a taxi to brake hard allowing the car behind it to drive into his rear. The onslaught of car horns then caught Mohammed's driver's eye who then decided to stop and run back to the incident to see if he could help. He recognised Barton lying prostrate on the road ..alive but obviously confused,

"Sir, sir are you ok?" the driver asked helping Barton to his feet.
"Come back to my car and we can take you to your hotel sir."
"Is President Mohammed in the car then?" asked Barton.
"Yes Sir."
On reaching the Mercedes Barton calmly jumped inside the back and took up his seat beside the surprised Brotherhood Leader,
"Thank goodness we met, Sir I have just been upstairs to find you" Dick pointed out.
"What is it Group Captain?"
"I really cannot tell you definitely it's just a feeling , not a good one Sir, but something is brewing.....it could be an attack on you. It's just a feeling" Barton advised Mohammed.
The tall Egyptian took time to consider his friend's concern,
"I do appreciate your advising me of this my friend but I cannot alter my daily schedule on that. Can I drop you here?"

Suitably rested Piratin gathered his wits, got dressed and proceeded to the briefing room beside the main hanger for the latest weather reports. All the remaining seven crew were in attendance as he entered the compact room from the peacefulness of the early evening air. The Met (meteorological) officer was already sat at his desk. Piratin took his seat and in walked General Samsonite who took the assembly,

"Good evening gentlemen. Hope you are suitably rested. I can report that your planes are full and armed to the teeth with 2000 pounders. Latest satellite intel shows no expectation of your arrival at your targets. The Lieutenant will now give you the latest and predicted weather over Egypt."

The lieutenant's delivery was brief as the conditions would be perfect for the early morning attack.

The 24hr wall clock displayed 1725hrs. Time for the crews to board the waiting B-2's. Up to this point Piratin had been so engrossed in his duties he had failed to notice the long flowing blonde hair of Major Grey but walking up his aircraft , for the first time in the last twelve or hours, she had not yet donned her helmet.

Having been entirely dedicated to his career, marriage and women in general, had not played a major role in the Colonel's life. To have attained the rank of full Colonel in his thirties there had been a price to pay. He had flown with Grey on several sorties and to this point had treated her as one of the boys, but something about the blonde hair, gently flowing in the evening breeze caught his attention!

"Concentrate Piratin, you are on the most important mission of your life" he kept muttering to himself under his breath,

"After you Major" he beckoned her up the cockpit steps.

All was set: the on-board stopwatch read 1748hrs, the pre-start up checks were complete, the navigation computers fully programmed and weapons systems tested and primed.

Piratin called the remaining three' birds' for approval to start,

"Ok Major?"

"Yes sir"

"Death Squadron to Fairford tower. Ready for start" he requested of the tower control.

"You are go for start up sir. Time 1758hrs Zulu."

The serenely quiet Gloucestershire airfield became enveloped in the high pitched B-2 engine wine as all sixteen General Electric's sprang into life spooling up to idle power.

"Death Squadron to tower request taxy"

called Piratin.
"Tower to Death Squadron. Clear to taxy to runway 09R. Wind 120 degrees six kts."
The engine notes changed as each aircraft spooled up to taxy power and made it's way to the threshold of 09R.
As before a box formation take-off had been agreed. All checks complete and flight plan approved,
"Death Squadron. Ready for take-off" called Piratin.
"You are clear to go Sir. Hit them hard sir..good luck. See you all back in twelve hours" replied the senior controller.
"You can do the take-off Major" ordered Piratin.
"I have control" she replied and plunged the four throttles to the max.
Totally unbeknown to the crews of all B-2A's their presence at Fairford had not gone unnoticed amongst the local plane spotter community several of whom had gathered at the end of the runway in the hope of capturing some photos.
80, 100,130, 170 kts *"Vi, rotate ..V2"* called out Piratin as Grey pulled back on the stick,
"Good climb gear up" he continued and raised the undercarriage.
As the climbing B-2A, struggling for height

under the huge weight of the payload, reached the far end of the runway passing one hundred and fifty feet the noise was shattering. The waiting plane spotters were taken by surprise as to the sheer roar and volume of the engine exhaust sending most of them to the vibrating ground holding their hands firmly over their ears! and then to be repeated three more times ..ecstasy for the photo fanatics!
Soon the sixteen black trails led far away into the deep blue eastern evening sky

........The B-2A 'Death Squadron'
was on it's way to war.

Barton arrived back at the King Tut and having ascended the vast flights of filthy stairs crashed out on his bed for a rest and quiet think.
He felt certain that MI6 knew more than they were telling him in the e-mails. The thought of an attack on Cairo ran paramount amongst the various ideas running through his head... but why? Why would UK attack Cairo? Then the penny dropped as his mind wandered three thousand miles west of London .. *"Of course The States. It was they who would be crazy enough to launch a first*

strike" he mumbled in his semi-conscious state. If true then his first priority was to get out of Cairo, but where to? The Group Captain fell asleep.

Two and a half hours since the squadron had departed the cool English countryside at Fairford and were presently cruising at Flight Level 45 (45,000 feet). Holding a southerly heading had brought them to the MATZ (Military Air Traffic Zone) of Gibraltar where Piratin would alter their course to 075 degrees taking them over the waters of the warm Mediterranean towards Sardinia.
The view of the Spanish coast below was nothing but majestic in the cloudless night sky. The extent of their altitude allowed all the pilots a grandstand observation of the town lights of Gibraltar, Marbella and Fuengirola in Spain and Tangier in Morocco.
The monotony of the flight to Gibraltar had given Piratin ample opportunity to converse with the beautiful Major Grey and managed to establish that she had been married, divorced and as luck would have it, now looking for some fun time. Raised in Sarasota, Florida she went straight to the Air Force Academy from Miami University, then like so many other service personnel her

civilian husband did not understand the military commitment.
"*Death 1 to all. Sardinia in 15 then alter to 165 degrees. Full radio silence from now*" Piratin informed the other three B-2A's.
Dead on schedule, with two hundred miles to run to Egyptian airspace, the time had come for the Squadron to split and take their independent routes to target.
One by one the 'flying wings' peeled away from the formation. Major Derrick altered the course of 'Spirit of Florida' to 145 degrees for his target of the air base at Al Mansurah on the Med coast, Major Fox altered 'Spirit of Texas' to 155 degrees towards his target of the air base at Fayid on the Sinai border and Major Andersen altered ' Spirit of Indiana' to 160 degrees for his target of the air base of Inshas in the Nile Basin whilst Piratin maintained his 165 degrees directly for Cairo.

Passing overhead the island of Crete with the lights of Heraklion clearly visible, the comms board of 'Spirit of New York' began to emit a blue light, underneath of which was written "Auth". Major Grey turned to Piratin,
"*It's the final go Sir. We have just received it.*"
"*Very well* " Piratin acknowledged. A few

moments of silence passed before she once again turned to her boss,
"Sir do you not feel a little scared??
He was quick to reply,
"Major I would be worried if I was not a little."
Again silence reigned for the next few minutes before Piratin uttered his next order to Grey,
"Ok, we are at our alpha point reduce altitude to five hundred feet and speed to four hundred."
Whilst the other three B-2A's were to drop their payloads from altitude taking full advantage of the stealth profile presented by the B-2A, Colonel Piratin had elected to go in low, very low. He had his reasons and was not about to share them.
Skimming over the calm Mediterranean water at around nine miles a minute concentrated the mind especially as the lights of El-Alamein on the Egyptian coast sprang into view. The TFR (Terrain Following Radar) aboard the B-2A was superb but the crew needed to be able to take over from the management computer at a second's notice should something go wrong.
"Ok Major we are on the final run into Cairo time to activate the payload and open the

bomb doors please" commanded Piratin.
"Confirmed Sir, and full radar jam operational. GPS (Global Positioning System) is fully interrogated and weapons nav computers correctly programmed."
"Excellent, keep your eye on the passive (radar) for any high-speed traffic or SAM's" continued Piratin.
The cool, flat, virtually uninhabited desert flashed beneath them with the aircraft gently vibrating as the weak remains of the day's thermals rose from the sand.
"Cairo dead on the nose Colonel" Grey pointed out as the unmistakable mass of light lit up the sky.
"Keep calling out the track mods and launch countdown please" he asked of Grey.
Due to it's sophisticated aerodynamic design and low power setting to hold four hundred kts the noise issued by the huge aircraft as it passed over several small villages was minimal. Few, if any of the villagers were disturbed from their sleep.
"4 degrees port, 35" the Major called out.
"25, 20, 15, 2 more degrees port, 10, 5, 4, 3, 2" and before she called 1 Piratin instructed the computer to initiate release.
Both crew could sense the two rotary cages revolving as they released each of the Mk84

2000 pounders in turn.
"All gone sir" Grey called out as Piratin plunged the throttles fully forward, closed the bomb doors and pulled the stick back into a hard starboard climb to height. Now he wanted to encompass the full stealth profile of ' New York' by getting back to FL 45 as soon as he could. The noise below was shattering awakening every soul in Cairo!
Booom!, Booom!, Booom! as each bomb plastered into it's target ...Tahrir Square, with the main Mogamma building on the southern end being the primary target. Colossal amounts of debris was thrown into the air as the huge balls of red and yellow flame turned to a rising billowing cloud of smoke.
The centre of Cairo had had it's heart ripped out as acres now lay in rubble and ruin, but had they got Nasil Mohammed and his Council as intel had led them to believe they were in residence in the Mogamma that very night.
A similar scene was beheld at the three airfields where the Egyptian Air Force had been taken completely by surprise. All three now lay in ruin with a possible two hundred and fifty fighter aircraft destroyed.

Piloted by Mulazim Awwal (Flying Officer) Amasis the lone F-16 fighter jet was returning to Inshas Air Base from a solo night training sortie over Aswan when Amasis was faced with several balls of flames rising into the Cairo air. As a junior twenty four year old Officer still under pilot training on the single engined F-16 he could not figure out what could have happened, maybe a gas explosion went through his mind. But then, in the distance he observed three more flumes of fire rise to the heavens in the dark sky.
This was no gas problem he now thought .. must be Israel invading? Pushing his throttle forward and engaging full afterburner Amasis instinctively climbed for height. As he passed FL 25 in the vertical with nothing showing on his air-to-air radar, before him appeared this huge black strange shaped 'wing'!
Normally Egyptians do not swear but on this occasion the F-16 pilot shouted out,
" Kuss Ummark" (Fuck you or slightly worse) as he fought to avoid a collision.
"American!" he then exclaimed recognising the aircraft.
"Colonel we have a echo on the scope. Small

and fast and very, very close!" shouted Grey. What could Piratin do than to continue in the climb.
Amasis completed a loop to bring him up and under the B-2A before loosing of his two sidewinder missiles. Both struck home in the rear of the B-2A tearing massive chunks out of the rear assembly and port wing before either Piratin or Grey could discharge their chaff (aerial countermeasures),
"We've been hit Major. Control is almost useless. Will head for the sea for a ditch" shouted the Colonel. Both pilots fought like devils to control the almost uncontrollable B-2A . Attempting to hold a northerly course which they knew would eventually bring them over water, their height was degrading at four thousand feet a minute. Smoke was billowing from the aircraft's rear and the port engines began to surge.
The fight to keep the aircraft under some form of control was becoming intolerable, the noise and vibration was so intense,
"We will hold on as long as we can but prepare to eject. I will give the order for you to go first Major but we must make the sea" shouted Piratin at the top of his voice.
With one hundred per cent power being delivered from the starboard engines but

only a surging twenty to twenty five per cent from the port the combination of the computers and crew could not hold a straight course. Piratin had no alternative than to reduce the port power and accept the steeper descent in order to avoid the possibility of entering a spin,

"I have the sea Colonel at about ten miles" shouted Grey.

"What's our height?" asked Piratin.

"Four thousand five hundred!"

"Just make it then!"

Bang! as the first port engine exploded which in turn took out the other port engine. The descent path sharpened yet again.

"Get ready Major and may God be with you!" shouted Piratin. The water came up fast. They could smell it now,

"Hold it, hold it, hold it now! Eject Major! Eject eject."

The cockpit filled smoke and an inordinate amount of noise as the cockpit roof was blown away microseconds before Grey's seat thrusters ignited rocketing the co-pilot and her seat skyward at one hundred g +. No sooner than she had cleared the aircraft Piratin pulled his yellow and black handle between his legs igniting his rocket packs.

The cool night air and encompassing silence

quickly awoke the temporary unconscious Colonel only to find himself hanging from his parachute straps just feet from the water. ..then splash! as he sank to around ten feet before rising to the surface with the aid of his life vest. The whole ejection procedure was fully automatic..all he had to do now was to survive!.

The massive silky white parachute lay motionless on the sea surface impeding Piratin's access to fresh air as his body rose, only to surface under the material.

The water was cold and together with the shock of the whole experience drew all of the fit man's endeavours to free himself from the ceiling of material.

Eventually he saw the star lit sky and for the first time in many seconds was able to breath normally.

"Are you ok Colonel, are you ok?" he heard in the distance. It was the softness of a familiar female voice that brought a sense of relief to him.

"Yes I'm fine." It was the Major.

Focussing his attention in the direction of the voice Piratin could make out a small circular, bright orange object with a canvas roof ..it was the life-raft with Major Grey relentlessly paddling towards him.

" *Grab my hand Sir"* she called out.
With great difficulty the experienced pilot managed to climb aboard and relaxed into the arms of his delightful co-pilot. The tight space within the single man raft was somewhat restricted, but then Piratin did not complain.
Ten minutes passed to rest and regain their strength and composure from the dramatic events of their ejection procedure before either spoke. The boss was the first to do so,
"Ok first things first. Radio." Packed tightly in a waterproof pocket of the raft was the emergency kit containing such items as emergency transmitter, torch, water, food, medical kit and foil sheets plus a pack of four flares.
There was only one frequency locked into the microtransmitter, that of the emergency distress of the US Military.
With the transmitter successfully engaged the two seamen agreed their position to be ten miles off the Egyptian coast just north of Alexandria. What was of concern was that they calculated the tide to be taking them shoreward!
The moment the emergency signal was emitted 'Death's two, three and four', who had managed to re-formate well clear of

Egyptian airspace over the sea, picked up the signal and now realised that 'Death One' had ditched into the water. To all of their utter frustration there was nothing they could do to assist their Squadron Leader other than re-confirm to Whiteman Air Base by breaking radio silence, via satellite comms, of the situation.

The panic and confusion left in central Cairo was simply out of control. Despite being in possession of Barton's premonition, Mohammed had not enacted upon it. The general public of Cairo had absolutely no idea of the political tension surrounding them and to find the centre and very heart of their city completely destroyed was beyond their comprehension. To their benefit the attack was carried out in the early hours of the morning when most people were at home in the suburbs fast asleep. Had it come during the day the casualty level would have climbed into the many thousands, but what of Nasil Mohammed and the rest of the Council?

Only time would reveal!

On hearing and feeling the continual explosions as the 2000 pounders made contact Barton had leapt from his bed in his

underwear and taken flight down the stairway to the basement of the building.where he joined several other staff and occasional guest. He had survived the onslaught.
It was clear for all those gathered in the dark cellar to hear Barton shout out in English,
"You fucking idiots in Washington. Did you not realise what this would now do!!! You total arsoles!!"
Many of those huddling together understood English.

The Base Commander at Whiteman was devastated to hear of the demise of 'Death one' and immediately ordered the assistance of the Navy to utilise it's nearest ship to Piratin's position to locate and recover the pilots with the utmost haste.

Chapter Eight

..."Repercussions"

News of this adverse nature travels at light speed and before the remains of 'Death Squadron' had cleared the Bay of Biscay (north Spain) en-route back to RAF Fairford to re- fuel for their trip back to Whiteman, the world press went crazy with newsflashes appearing the world over.
Air Marshal Brian Hendersen was hurriedly dispatched by the Prime Minister to Fairford to meet and interrogate the returning crews whilst he, himself, lifted the RED telephone to Washington.
O'Shea was fast asleep when Feldman's call was put through and was not best pleased with Feldman's irate attitude. Following the heated discussion of several minutes both agreed to meet at the earliest opportunity which Feldman suggested might be a NATO or United Nations Security Council meeting

which was sure to be convened by Robert Kuok, the United Nations Secretary General.

Hendersen, having been chauffeur driven in the Prime Minister's Jaguar car from Whitehall to Gloucestershire, arrived at the main gate to RAF Fairford in time to see the three huge B-2A's touch down in the early morning light in a line astern formation, only to be refused entry by the American Duty Sergeant. Under considerable pressure from a very senior officer Sergeant Diaz made contact with Lieutenant General Samsonite's office to inform him of the Air Marshal's arrival.

"Jesus man let him in and escort the Air Marshal to my office, now!" shouted the General.

Hurriedly Samsonite got dressed into his uniform, although still unshaved and ungroomed, to greet Hendersen. The meeting was frosty but respectful. The ending did not please the Air Marshal as he was denied permission to see the crews who now, albeit very concerned of the situation with Colonel Piratin and Major Grey, were resting in the Officers mess.

Hendersen left to report back to the PM.

Of all the terrorist groups throughout the Middle-East that were willing to give their name and signature to the, now lost '**Peace Agreement**', it was Ahmad Habib of Hamas who displayed the greatest anger at the surprise attack on Egypt.
Rarely seen in the public media he immediately called a press meeting to be held in his Gaza Office to vent his opinion of the actions taken by the American President.

During this time of upheaval and political wrangling, and soon to be military reprisals, the hunt for Speedbird 4674 had been continuing, but to no avail.

For the time being O'Shea took the criticism of his actions from Habib. He (O'Shea) was a politician and only delivered his punch lines when certain they would have the greatest effect. The revelations of the arms in the tunnels and the invoice would come soon enough. The call he was expecting came through, .. from Jacob Benayoun.
Having been kept in the dark as to the surprise attack, the Israeli Prime Minister took glee in it's announcement and rang

O'Shea for a possible commentary on what else might be planned. There was nothing else to be advised of except to expect Hamas to take advantage and launch an attack on Israel at any time. Benayoun took the point. They agreed to be in daily contact for the next week or so.

The same understanding attitude could not be attributed to the various Islamic fundalmentalistic factions throughout the Middle-East. The phone lines between Damascus, Beirut, Gaza and what was left of the underground Brotherhood movement in Cairo were hot but of more concern to the stability of the world was the rising interest shown by several new but excessively violent groups, namely ; Isil in Iraq, Boko Haram in Nigeria, Al-Shabaab in East Africa, Al Qaeda in Pakistan and Al-Nusra in central Africa.

What O'Shea had not allowed for in his rush to accuse The Egyptian Brotherhood of bringing down the British Airways aircraft was the joint reaction of these hitherto unconnected groups.

Without doubt all the leaders of these groups were itching to strike back at the Imperialistic West, namely the United States and those who supported them, but none would make the first move in fear of being in

receipt of the treatment that Cairo had just experienced. They were all just waiting for the curtain to open for the performance to begin.
They did not have long to wait as two days after the Cairo incident, just as The Security Council of the United Nations was about to convene, all hell broke out in the towns of Ofakim, Rohat and Nevtivot in the open strip between Israel and Gaza.
Habib had persuaded his Hamas brothers on an all out first strike. He felt the time was right and that Arab opinion would be with him.
With thousands of fighters, outfitted in their traditional black, pouring into the extensive tunnel system, unaware that the tunnel at Nevtivot had been compromised, the attack was to be within hours.
The final strategy of "take no prisoners" issued by Habib was passed down the ranks. All was ready, until it was discovered that the Israeli's had destroyed one of the arms stashes at Nevtivot, but it was too late to postpone the advance at this stage thought Habib and ordered the attack to begin.
At the tunnel exits they had discovered the Israeli forces were patiently lying in wait, however, there were many, mainly in the

north leading towards the town of Qiryat Gat, they had not found.
As arranged on the hour of 1800hrs, just as the darkness was beginning to fall, all tunnels were broken through the Israeli soil. First out were two waves of soldiers fully armed with AK-47's and RPG's whose task was to securify the near area to enable the mechanised force of Russian BTR-60PB's with single gun turrets, Polish OT-64A's with single gun turrets and American M1114's with single gun turrets, to exit. Following the vehicles were the many thousands of individual fighters many of whom would be carrying the worst weapons of all .. chemical grenades!
At the Nevtivot and nearby exits not even the vehicles had a chance of escaping the tunnel confines as the intensive Israeli Merkava tank firepower brought the earth in upon them. It was a massacre in the making. Round upon round upon round of Israeli shells tore the tunnellers to shreds. It was a different story to the north where the Garzan and Hamas fighters found no resistance. Having broken through the undiscovered tunnels they rapidly consolidated their forces into two spearheads, one heading for

Jerusalem and the other for Tel Aviv.
Not relaxing into celebrating the success in the middle and southern strip, upon hearing the surprise news of the northern breakthrough, all tank divisions were immediately ordered north to intercept the Hamas breakthrough .. but the distance between them was considerable. Using latest intel the Commander in Chief of the Armed Forces rapidly directed the Air Force bases at Hatzor and Tel Nof to scramble all their
F-15 and F-16 fighter jets to attack and destroy the two spearheads.
News of their mixed results fed back to those of the Brotherhood that were still alive in Cairo. Colonel Piratin had done his job well.
Being themselves in a state of total disarray the remnants of the Brotherhood Council were in no position to go to Hamas's aid especially as more than half their Air Force had just been destroyed. Habib was on his own and with much of his force having been wiped out at Nevtivot did not stand a chance against the air onslaught that was to be delivered by several squadrons of F-15's and 16's. The forthcoming slaughter was inevitable. Many found their way back to Gaza through the tunnels but it was calculated that around four thousand nine

hundred would never see their homeland again.
This long and extensively planned attack on Israel had blatantly and embarrassingly failed.

The confines of the small raft and the lack of anything else to do than to talk, had brought Piratin and Grey closer together. Re-grading to Christian names in their conversation was a clear sign. Ejecting out of a B-2 Stealth bomber put them into a singularly unique club of which they were the only two members. That would foster a relationship between them for life.
The USS Alabama, one of the Arleigh Burke class destroyers based in the Mediterranean was the first ship to pick up the distress signal and having sought permission from the Fleet Commander, altered to a south-easterly course .
The dark still night plus the relative calmness of the sea and their relaxed demeanour from the furore of battle soon saw the drifting couple kissing, however a chance glance from Piratin's eye caught a glint on the horizon,
" Caroline look did you see that?" pointing towards the Egyptian shoreline.
"No. What did you see?" asked Major Grey.

"Not sure but could have been a torch which means a search party" Piratin suggested. *"Better get our pistols out"* he continued. Sure enough as the first hour just turned into the second there in the darkness, silhouetted against the deep blue morning sky, they both saw the shape of five small patrol boats heading straight at them.
"*We do not stand a chance !"* yelled Caroline Grey, *"They must have twenty soldiers on all those boats."*
"We must fight and die is necessary as the alternative capture and torture and public humiliation would be worse" continued Piratin.
Multiple shots rang out from the Egyptian launches several of which hit the life raft. It started to deflate. Both fired back but in vane. Two small calibre side-arms were of no consequence against such odds but still they unleashed both magazines until, 'click, click'. The chambers were empty.
"Sir, sir I have several echoes at three kilometres at 165 degrees directly in line with the signal" shouted out the radar operative aboard the Alabama.
Immediately the Captain ordered full power to twenty eight knots and the preparation to

launch two high-speed ribs.
"Fuck, fuck !!" shouted Piratin, *"We should have saved two bullets for us!"*
The life-raft had completely deflated and enveloped the two B-2A pilots as it still maintained floatation.
Two of the launches drew alongside what was left of the rubber raft and hoisted the exhausted prisoners aboard.
"Launch the ribs, now Lieutenant " ordered the Captain as he made out the action unfolding before him through his powerful binoculars..
"Aye Aye sir" and away they went, within seconds, at their full speed of thirty two kts.
"Sir we have company. Two high-speed boats approaching from the north west" rang out the scope reader on the lead launch.
"Very well, we three craft will intercept them. Tell the other two to get those prisoners back to Alexandria at any cost!" ordered the Patrol Commander who altered the course of his three boat flotilla towards the incoming American ribs.
Within minutes shots were exchanged as the boats drew closer. The first casualty was one of the Egyptian boats which disintegrated when the American RPG shell scored a direct hit. The success was short lived as the closer

of the inflatable ribs took a strafing of machine gun bullets down it's port side. It was now two against two. Exchanges of fire continued as all three darted in and out of a circle of confusion in the lightening dawn until the remaining American rib and Egyptian leading launch collided in a blinding flash. The attempt by the crew of the Alabama to recover their countryman had failed. Piratin and Grey were now prisoners of war incarcerated in the Brotherhood's temporary HQ in central Alexandria.
There could be now no doubt throughout the world that the all important
'**Peace Agreement**' was now well and truly dead!

The drums had started beating loud amongst the various terrorist groups with Al-Malouf, the self appointment leader of the Syrian Freedom Movement, calling for a concerted joint Fatwa against the United States and Israel and to include those Shi'a muslims that side with and had a liking of the western way of life. If accepted by the other groups then this would indeed be an all out religious war on a grand scale!
To this end Al-Malouf ordered all his loyal forces into the Dayr Az Zawr region of

eastern Syria and called for the new Islamic Caliphate of IC to be sanctified and he himself to be appointed as the Caliph. His vision was to expand IC outwards into Iraq, Lebanon, Gaza, Egypt and eventually Iran to complete the new Caliphate.
The call was being answered as many Sunni's embarked on their homage to east Syria. From as far as Egypt and remote parts of Iran to the foothills of the Golan Heights, even from the suburbs of Birmingham, UK, the loyalists travelled to the call of the new IC.

The darkness of the cell was soon brightened by the shaft of light beaming in the Egyptian sunshine as the door opened. In walked three soldiers and roughly manhandled both Colonel Piratin and his co-pilot to their feet,
"You come with us" shouted one of the soldiers in a broken English.
At first the bright morning light forced the Americans to squint their eyes but once acclimatised they appreciated they were in an old building.
"Take them in there."
The room was dark with the one window blacked out by a torn and tatty curtain. There two chairs facing a desk behind which sat the

silhouette of an elderly man wearing a forage cap. Piratin took him to be military.
"Stand them over there in front of the chairs" ordered the man in Egyptian before he changed to English,
" My name is Ally. You are American?" he asked.
"Piratin, Colonel 287543."
"Grey, Major 872356."
" Colonel we all know that you were the pilots of that incredible machine that just bombed my country. Now we can do what I want the easy way or difficult way. You will both be interviewed on television and you will both unreservedly apologise for bombing Cairo and admit that your country was totally in the wrong to have ordered you to do it. Will you do that?" Ally asked.
Silence! Silence!
Piratin and Grey merely looked at each other with a sense of despair and inevitability in their eyes.
"Very well Colonel, Major, let's have some fun and see if I can change your mind."
Gesticulating at the two soldiers, they manhandled Piratin several feet away from Grey and turned him to face her.

"Take a seat and enjoy the show Colonel" spoke Ally in a soft but happily condescending manner as he slipped the chair behind the American Colonel.
"We Egyptians have no need of physical persuasion..psychological is much more effective Mr. American ..you will see" advised Ally walking over to the beautiful
Ms Grey.
"Allah has sent me a gift on this occasion" he continued, *"a female pilot and so beautiful. I wonder how your training will handle this!"*
Of a similar height to Caroline Grey allowed Ally to lean forward, put his arms around her slim body and attempt to kiss her. Grey tried in vain to repel the blagard with the garlic infested breath but his enormously strong arms held her tight. The kiss continued for many seconds. Piratin wanted so much to rise and kill the Egyptian pig but the two thugs behind him were all to eager to restrain him. Piratin sat and watched.
As Ally withdrew from the embrace Grey deposited an inordinately large amount of spit in his face.
Leaving it to run down his cheeks," *So you enjoyed that then! Let's go further"* Ally spoke.

"Take off your flying suit Major, now!" he ordered in a loud and authoritative voice as he wiped the spit from his face.
"Get fucked you bastard" Grey shouted.
"Oh I intend too soon, thank you for the offer!" Ally responded.
Grey's shaking body just stood there eyeballing the Egyptian. Not wishing to waste time Ally grabbed the flight suit zipper and yanked it down to her crutch. Then grasping the shoulder epaulettes violently pulled the suit off her shoulders allowing it to fall to Grey's feet.
There she stood in her pretty white bra and panties. Piratin felt a sense of dangerous excitement dwelling within his loins but what could he do?
"Are you ready now Colonel?" Ally asked.
Silence.
"Very well. Get me the scissors Sergeant" Ally asked of the senior soldier.
The denigration of Grey continued. Ally fondled the long blonde hair whilst clicking the scissors.
"No ! " shouted Piratin.
"Are you ready to cooperate Colonel?" asked Ally.
"Don't give in Sir" cried Grey as tears began

to trickle down her cheek. Silence.
Snip as the first lock was cut from her head. And another, and another until what was left was just a few stubs of growth.
Still silence.
"I am getting impatient Colonel!"
Silence.
Ally then walked behind the shivering
Ms Grey. Snip, snip as the scissors cut through her bra straps.
"Enough Colonel? Shall I continue?" It was at this point that the yellow liquid trickled down Grey's inside leg.
"I'm so sorry Major" Piratin murmured.
Then silence.
Snip, snip as the scissors cut through either side of her panties. They dropped to the ground adding to the ungainly pile of the flying suit, bra and blonde hair.
Ally waited for a response from the American Colonel ..none came.
"Very well Colonel. Crunch time" beckoning the junior soldier to come over and stand behind Grey.
"Bend over beautiful American pilot" Ally commanded of Grey in a loud voice.
"Get stuffed you fucking bastard" shouted Grey.
"I'm not but you are. Soldier take your

trousers and pants down" ordered Ally as he physically forced Grey to bend over holding her head down with both hands.

With his third leg standing to attention the soldier stood there as his face gained a rudy complexion in a mixture of embarrassment and excitement.
"Go ahead soldier, now!" commanded Ally.
The nervous soldier crept forwards and was just about to insert when Piratin took to his feet but was immediately pushed back down by the burly Sergeant,
"Ok, ok, ok stop it stop it now, you win. I will say it" moaned the Colonel.
A rather disappointing smile crept across Ally's face,
"Excellent I knew you would come round in the end Colonel. Put your trousers back on soldier and get out."

Across the Atlantic the President's satisfaction over a mission well done was marred by his deep concern for the loss of a B-2A, costing two billion dollars but more so for the demise of the two crew. The skipper of the Alabama had relayed the news of Piratin's capture to the White House. He

(the President) was glad of the safe arrival of the other three aircraft at Whiteman Air Base. All that was now expected by the Senate was the political fall-out and anti-American reteric from the Islamic world. Better that, thought O' Shea, than the possible destruction of Israel. What he, or the Senate, did not prepare for was the incoming news bulletins of the gathering together of so many terrorist groups in Syria. The sketchy intel announcement of the formation of a new Caliphate had been way beyond their expectations. A new and potentially much more dangerous threat would now be focussing their minds!

Apart from a private venture exploration ship monitoring in the Mid-Atlantic the complete search for BA 4674 was non-existent. The loss would be put down as a Bermuda Triangle type mystery. In this vane the 'Peace Agreement' had well and truly vanished beyond rescue.

With considerable pressure being brought to bear on O'Shea from 'Special Services' a black ops rescue plan to extract the captured B-2A crew had been sanctioned. It was important for the nation's morale that all servicemen were to be brought home, whatever the cost. The plan would be complex and risky and a team of twenty volunteers from the USN Seals special forces presently based on-board the USS Alabama would be sought.

Meanwhile a squadron of U2 extremely high altitude spy planes had been dispatched to RAF Fairford with the mission of photo-reconnaissance over Syria and Iraq. The movements of terrorist groups within the alleged Caliphate was to be recorded in the greatest detail and analysed.

The following day President O'Shea was abruptly disturbed during his daily staff meeting by his PPS,
"Sir, sir sorry to disturb but you must switch on CNN" she shouted. Immediately O'Shea rushed across the room to pick up the remote control and depressed 'on'.
The sixty inch plazma screen hanging on the wall burst into life displaying the two B-2A pilots.
"What the?" exclaimed O'Shea as he displayed anger at seeing his military being paraded on what now he considered third world television.

Major Grey, fully dressed in her fly suit unzipped to just below her breasts and with her stubbled hair, was crying but silent. Colonel Piratin with multiple bruises clearly visible on his face was talking into the microphone placed on the table at which he was sitting,

"....... apologise for my countries action in bombing Cairo."

During his brief deliberation the staff in the Oval Room understood the code that Piratin was saying with the occasional rubbing of his fingers under his nose. It signified that they were under severe duress and had said nothing.

"So you personally apologise for your attack on our beloved city Colonel?" asked the Egyptian interviewer.

"Y.....yes."

The interviewer then took the microphone,

"America. You may have these two back when you send us twenty billion dollars to rebuild our city. We give you one week."

The screen went blank.

The Secretary of State spoke,

"I know Colonel Piratin. Good man but the girl .... we must get them home Mr. President."

"It's all underway Larry" replied O'Shea.

Chapter Nine

..."Build up to War"

The Alabama's Seal team, led by Captain De Loratio, landed safely undetected on the dark, deserted Egyptian beach just a few hundred yards west of El-Alamein. Having covered the four rib boats with a blend of tree branches, sand and seaweed the platoon set

off the find the Alex-Marsa Matouh Road at the top of the beach.
Two or three cars passed as the team hid in the undergrowth, then Sergeant Arico, the advanced spotter, whispered in his radio,

"Lorry 10 secs."
As the headlights slowly approached one of the Seals stepped out into the middle of the sandy, potholed road and waving the driver down. As soon as the lorry had stopped the driver had a 5.56mm M4A1 assault muzzle pushed into his face.
With the driver securely bound and gagged before being dragged away from the main road out of sight, the Seal team climbed aboard the truck and headed for Alexandria which lay some twenty kilometres away to the east.
The location of Colonel Piratin and his co-pilot were known to De Loratio at all times due to the micro implant short range transmitter sewn into the gusset of the flying suits of all front line pilots. According to Captain De Loratio's GPS both pilots were together in the southern suburbs of the city. Without much difficulty they could drive straight up to the front door! After all no-one was expecting them..the cover offered by the

lorry was perfect, it even had vegetable delivery written on the side.
The building in Al Narges Str was a two storey mud/brick terraced construction with a roof terrace. An easy property for a covert entry, thought De Loratio, but to do it without creating noise and disturbing those sleeping in the street would not be so easy. He ordered half his force to use pistols with silencers attached to join him and gain the first entry into the building whilst the rest would set in a security perimeter carrying their assault rifles. Picking the front door lock De Loratio crept into the corridor and was immediately faced with two very surprised men whom he instinctively, shot dead! Rapidly the balance of his team, in utter silence, took possession of each ground floor room all of which they found empty.
Holding five fingers aloft and pointing up the stairs De Loratio led the assault force to the first floor. It was his weight on the very last step that emitted the loud creak in the otherwise dead evening silence bringing one of the captors to the door to investigate. On realising that the perpetrators were in uniform and therefore not Egyptian the thug started to cry out only to be stopped when De

Loratio's bullet entered his throat. The others resting in the room heard the muted cry and consequent thud as the body hit the floor and ran for their pistols ..in vain as the Seals entered the room and opened fire first. The five bodies lay bleeding on the floor. The door opposite then opened, " Thug, thug" as several bullets left the Seal's pistol sending the captor to the floor. On entering the second room the Seals found the two pilots sitting on the floor bound and gagged together,
"*Colonel, I'm De Loratio. We have come to take you both home*" he whispered as one of the seals cut the bonds with his razor sharp stiletto knife.
"Oh boy are we glad to see you Captain. Be careful with Major Grey. It's been rough for her" stated the smiling Colonel.
In their hurry to vacate the house the team neglected to observe the small movement from one of the captors lying in the corridor. The team, led by De Loratio closely followed by Colonel Piratin then Major Grey, started down the stairs. As the last man's foot hit the creaking stairboard the wounded captor raised his pistol and fired getting the Seal in the back. The Seal fell forwards down the stairs taking several others with him, except

for Sergeant Arico who turned and shot the thug in the head.
The sound of the unmuffled shot rang loud down Al Narges Str awakening many of the residents who looked out of their windows only to see a team of armed soldiers jumping into a lorry. The men in number 4, 8 and 14 Al Narges Str stirred from their sleep and had the alertness to grab their pistols and fire at the Seals. Two took rounds in their shoulders before several of the other Seals raised their M4A1's and let lose with several hundred rounds killing all three residents,
"Go, go come on drive man let's get out of here" shouted De Loratio.
The lorry hit sixty by the end of the road, almost turning over as it turned into the next street as the driver headed back in the night to the Alex-Marsa Matouh Road.
On arrival back at the beach De Loratio could see several headlights speeding towards them from Alexandria.
"Must be the army Sir" Arico suggested.
"Yep. Take five men and set up a reception committee whilst I get the boats back in the water" ordered the Captain.
Firing broke out just as the first boat hit the water,
"Get in Sir and you Major, these boys will

get you back to the Alabama whilst we take care of these suckers" De Loratio commanded. The two rib boats with ten souls which included the freed prisoners and wounded, pushed out to sea.

The firing became much more intense as the lights bore down upon the beach, then **pow**! as the first RPG exploded amidst the Seals grouped together near the remaining boats. All but two were killed instantly. Their time came seconds later as the second grenade exploded, then the third and forth.
The firing ceased.

"Welcome aboard Colonel and you Major. Come below and get warm and have some food" greeted Commander O'Brian.
"Shortly Commander, I am concerned about Captain De Loratio and the rest of your Seals. I am not sure they made it. The fire battle we saw in the dark was too intense for anyone to survive" advised Piratin.
"We gathered that Colonel" whilst turning to his second in command the Commander shouted his order,
" Captain bear your guns on the beach and blow the Egyptian fuckers to hell."
Within seconds the large 5" Mk45 forward

mounted gun let rip with round after round. The beach area lit up with the multiple explosions as they piled into the sand and Marsa Road..
No-one survived.
From his chair in the Ward Room O'Brian swivelled round to face Alabama's Captain,
"Captain let's get the hell out of here."

The U2's photographic evidence brought back from their recent overflights of Syria had clearly shown the influx of thousands of so called Jihadists rallying to the new cause... the Caliphate.
This worrying scenario was of very grave concern to O'Shea, the Senate, Prime Minister Feldman and the United Nations amongst others. But what to do?
What was of really urgent concern to the American and Iraqi Presidents was the very latest U2 intel interpretation showing a vast IC force making it's way to the massive Mosul Dam, formerly known as the Saddam Dam, in northern Iraq. Should it fall into the Jihadists hands Baghdad, the capital city of Iraq, would be at their mercy. The mighty Mosul Lake containing eight and a half billion cubic metres of water is held back

from the River Tigris, whose course runs through Baghdad, by the huge dam. Should the dam be blown then Baghdad would be submerged under twenty feet of water killing an estimated half million people.

An emergency meeting of the United Nations Security Council was hurriedly convened for the following day.
The global exodus of those of a Sunni disposition wishing to join the new Caliphate grew from a trickle to became a torrent of humanity from as far as Central Africa and Australia. The several reports of severe violence undertaken by the Jihadists in pursuit of their acquisition of land was seeming to act as a magnet for all the thugs of the world who were getting misguided into what they thought to be a religious direction.
It would seem that no country was without it's gullible audience .. UK, France, Belgium, Sweden in particular all unwittingly supplied many followers of the self proclaimed IC leader, Al-Malouf. This young, radical Sunni Muslim who led the Syrian fighters against the brutality of President Gorani in the civil strife had seen fit to elevate his position to Caliph of the new Caliphate, IC.
The sacking of the Iraqi towns of Mosul and

Kirkuk acted as the turning point for the deluded many, willing to traverse the globe to become involved.
It became obvious from further American high altitude surveillance that the opposing forces in these towns yielded little resistance but more importantly took possession of many of the sophisticated military machinery donated to Iraq by the United States following the fall of Saddam Hussein.
With several thousand fanatical well armed Jihadists at their door the National Iraqi Protection Force, attributed with the order to protect the dam, stood little chance of success in preventing it's fall into IC hands. Very little blood was spilt in the battle as the Iraq soldiers were again quick to surrender when faced with such superior odds.
The jubilant Al-Malouf flushed with success wandered up and down the head of the Dam considering his next move. Receiving reports of the staggering numbers joining his cause seemed to impose an envelope of invincibility upon this ambitious young man. With the enormity of publicity the capture of the Dam would bring to the world's media, Al-Malouf thought this a good time to advise the world of his , thus far, unchallenged power.
A demonstration followed by an ultimatum

would be arranged for the following day.

The concern of the falling of the Mosul Dam angered President O'Shea to the point of him calling for an all out airbourne attack on IC. To a man and woman the Senate agreed with their President's wish and the Commanders in Chief of the armed forces were duly summoned to the White House to draw up their attack plans accordingly.

Dawn broke in the northern Iraqi desert throwing an ominous blood red cast across the undulating landscape.
Of the senior leadership that spent the night in the Iraqi Officers Quarters, Al-Malouf was the first to rise. His second in command, Wael Ayman Shaer, soon followed as he was to arrange the demonstration that his leader had called for.
The sun was well above the horizon as the fifty two Iraqi prisoners were marched out into the sunlight onto the Dam's breach where they were forced to kneel in a straight row. The video camera that was to film the event was securely mounted on a tripod facing the cowering Iraqis.
The stage was set beckoning the presence of

Al-Malouf who drew up to the proceedings in a captured American Hummer. With his head and face covered in a black silk scarf, but with a narrow slit for vision, to protect his identity he arrogantly walked over to the active camera and began the recording of his declaration in English,

"O'Shea this is a message for you. You bombed my brothers in Cairo and for this there is a price for you to pay. You will give twenty four billion dollars to Egypt by the end of this week to re-build the city. Should this not be paid by then I will blow this dam.You, or your United Nations friends will not interfere in any way with my plans to enlarge my Caliphate and as a lesson of what will happen to those I capture if you do, will now follow!"

He then took pride to display what he had been hiding behind his back during his delivery .. a large curved sword referred to as a scimitar.

Walking across to the first of the kneeling prisoners he raised the scimitar to shoulder height before bringing it swiftly down upon the poor soul's neck. The body slumped flat to the ground whilst the severed head rolled several feet forward.

The butcher repeated this performance a

further fifty one times!. The blood ran over the dam's edge and into the water below.
"There, learn from this lesson O'Shea!" The camera was switched off.

"You need to watch this youtube Mr. President. It was make you sick to your stomach Sir" advised his PPS (Personal Private Secretary). The sight of fifty two beheadings made O'Shea physically vomit onto the dark blue Oval Room carpet.
"When do we commence our bombing?" he turned and asked the PPS.
"*Tomorrow sir. The Med Fleet will be in theatre in the Gulf at 0800hrs tomorrow*" replied the PPS.
"Good I cannot wait to give those thugs a beating!"
"What are you going to do about the payment to Cairo Sir?" asked the PPS.
"Pay The Brotherhood twenty four billion ..never! We get those bastards before they blow the Dam, it's probably just a bluff anyway. Get Admiral Loran on-board the 'Gerald Ford' to watch that film and start his bombing around the Dam at 0805hrs!" ordered O'Shea.

Prime Minister Feldman also saw the

youtube video and like his Atlantic counterpart was sick to his stomach about it's contents. Not holding as powerful a position as the American President, Feldman anticipated an American intervention which he assumed would be followed by a cross-Atlantic request for the Royal Air Force to join in. As sickened as he was with the video this would not sit well with the British public he thought so to cover the possibility, Feldman requested an emergency NATO security conference be held in the UK at the earliest possible opportunity to discuss the deepening situation.

Time: 0825hrs.
Ship: American aircraft carrier Gerald Ford.
Location: Ten miles of Abadan, Iran in the Persian Gulf.

The first of the F-18 Super Hornet fighter jets left the carrier deck at one hundred and eighty kts with flames belching from both exhausts. The remaining five aircraft followed in quick succession.
Target: IC military emplacements around Mosul Dam.
Route: North across Iraq to Al Marah, Ba'Qubah and across the desert to Mosul.

Cruising at low altitude just under the sound barrier it would take the F-18 Squadron fifty five minutes to cover the one thousand kilometres. The burning stacks of the oil refinery at Abadan on the Iran/Iraq border, clearly visible to the pilots through the early morning mist, was the first positive check point for the aircraft before altering course for Al Marah.

"Eagle 1 to Squadron, five minutes to target. Arm payload" ordered the Squadron Commander.

The on-board advanced targeting infra-red radar could easily identify the defence emplacements and vehicle movements whose coordinates will be fed into the six AGM-25 Maverick missiles strapped under the wings of each F-18.

The Jihadist's were taken by complete surprise as the Super-Hornets appeared on the horizon just seconds before an array of missiles hit all fifteen machine gun emplacements blowing all those manning the guns to their maker. The remainder of the short time available for loitering gave the six aircraft the opportunity to use their 20mm Gatling guns to take out several vehicles and groups of people at will.

Literally seconds after first appearing all six F-18's were safely on their way back to the Gerald Ford.
As part of the overall planned strategy to secure the Dam, following the wave of American bombing, in would swoop two divisions of Kurdish and one of Iranian fighters from the northern most area of Iraq/ Iran called Kurdistan to take ground control and secure the Dam into friendly hands.

However, the overall numbers, the amount of weaponry and sheer ferocity of the fighting spirit of the IC overwhelmed the Kurdish/ Iranian Divisions who had no choice than to retreat leaving the Dam still under the control of IC.
The senior leadership of IC, including
Al-Malouf himself had managed to survive both onslaughts and on seeing the devastation wrought upon his fellow supporters vowed to take revenge. To this end he ordered the capture of four American humanitarian workers or journalists from the refugee camps on the Turkish border and for them to be transported to the Dam within twenty four hours. It was at this point, on

realising that Iranian fighters were involved in the skirmish against him that the furious Al-Malouf decided to eventually invade Iran and add that country to his Caliphate. Such a delusionary idea most would think crazy but then Al-Malouf was beginning to consider himself immortal.

Upon attending the de-brief from the returning F-18 pilots, Admiral Loran was surprised at the relative ineffectiveness of the combined attack on the Dam so immediately ordered another wave of six aircraft to get airborne and finish the job. Napalm, being a weapon on the UN prohibited list against use on civilian targets, was not usually the first choice in any commanders ordnance payload, but on this occasion with so much at stake Loran decided to order it's use.
The noise was shattering as one after the other the second wave of Super-Hornets left the Gerald Ford fully laden with a four hundred pound pod of napalm under each wing.

The sun was at it's zenith as the first of the F-18's swooped over the horizon at near supersonic speed at one hundred feet above the flat desert, however, on this occasion the

enemy was prepared!
The first batch of napalm pods hit their targets sited at the western end of the Dam resulting in the runs of liquid fire incinerating everything in their path. What was not known to the pilots was that all the IC men had been relocated to several new positions some five hundred metres to the south of the Dam.
The second and last batch hit the eastern targets leaving nothing but cinders when the fire-storm subsided.
The Squadron Commander somewhat in awe over the absence of return ground fire at his aircraft issued the 'return to base' order only to be interrupted by panic calls from nos. 5 and 6,
"No.5 Mayday, mayday I have missile lock on, I repeat missile lock on!!" shouted the pilot.
"No.6 Mayday mayday me too!" Both aircraft took drastic evasive action by going vertical, full left, full right on full afterburners but neither could shake off the incoming surface-to-air heat seeking missiles that Al-Malouf had captured from the Iraqi Army at Mosul!
One large mid-air explosion followed the other as the shoulder held FIM-92 Stingers

felled their prey from the sky. The pilot and navigator of the first aircraft managed to eject. Unfortunately the other aircrew never had time.
The remaining four jets now running low on fuel begrudgingly returned to the carrier in the Gulf.
Loran immediately reported the loss of his aircraft and possession of air missiles by IC back to the Pentagon and awaited further orders.

Al-Malouf sent out an armed escort to pick up the flight crew of the downed fighter jets. The two dead bodies of No. 6 were soon found and bundled into the back of the Hummer before speeding off into the desert to find the crew from No.5. It did not take long as several small arms fire rang out hitting the radiator grill of the Hummer, *"Just drive straight at them"* shouted the lead IC soldier,*" they only have revolvers and this car is bulletproof."*
The pilot and navigator could not offer much resistance to the car load of fully armed soldiers so were forced to stand high and raise their arms in surrender.
The four aircrew were thrown to the feet of

the waiting IC leader,
"You are American? Your President has delivered you to me. May Allah be blessed. You are going to be of great assistance to me" Al-Malouf told them.
"Get the video camera! and follow me outside" he then shouted to one of his men.
Some two hundred metres from the building stood a sole mud brick archway.
"Throw two ropes over the arch and hang up the two bodies and bring the two live ones and kneel them underneath" he ordered.
All was set for another gruesome video performance. Al-Malouf stood in front of the camera,
"Mister President of America. Instead of acceding to my earlier demand you dare to send more pilots to kill me. Big mistake. I have four of your boys here (camera pans to the two hanging) and now for the other two."
Turning to the kneeling aircrew Al-Malouf produced the scimitar and raised it high.
"No, no, no please no, not that . I hav...." the body slumped to the ground.
The pilot also pleaded,
"My wife and chil..." His head rolled some ten feet before coming to rest in

the sand.
The camera panned back to the IC leader ,
" Tomorrow I blow the Dam!"
The soldier uploaded the film onto youtube.com knowing full well that the CIA would pick it up in seconds.

The shouting from the White House could be heard in Pennsylvania Av as President O'Shea was shown the short video. The short period of unremitting rage then subdued into one of remorse as O'Shea and those in his office reflected on the situation and gave thought to the aircrews families.
Head in hands, the President sat at his desk in solace for several minutes. No-one spoke. A tear ran down O' Shea's cheek landing on the document beneath his elbows.
He looked up and stared each of those in the room, clean in the eye,
"Gentlemen, gentlemen this cannot go on like this. I will go to Feldman's NATO conference and call for an all out war. We are America. We will not be dictated to like this" and thumped the desk in anger.

Chapter Ten

..."WAR"

The only venue available, at such short notice, for the NATO conference was the Celtic Manor Hotel in Newport, Wales. A first class golf resort with a large commercial airport nearby at Cardiff allowing most of the twenty eight delegates to attend with the minimum of organisational effort. President O'Shea had elected to use Air Force One for

his Trans-Atlantic crossing and for added personal security would land at RAF Fairford lying only a few minutes flight time from Newport in a helicopter.
All was set for Tuesday 15th May. Security was to be very tight so some five thousand British police were to be drafted in from all over the UK, much to the inconvenience of the local community in Cardiff and Newport.
The huge Presidential Boeing 747-200 painted in two tone blue with polished aluminium engine exhaust nacelles touched down in the warm evening Gloucestershire air. Out stepped the sole figure of O'Shea closely followed by his official team. Patiently waiting for them just yards away on the dispersal pad was the Sikorsky UH-60 Blackhawk all warmed up and ready to fly the team to Newport.
With the various greeting salutations and photographic records completed the meeting began. It continued hour after hour with much heated debate but eventually in the late afternoon a vote was taken and unanimously passed for

...war against IC.

It had been agreed that the United Kingdom, France, Holland,and Germany would provide a joint air cover strike force of some sixty

three fighter jets to fly alongside the Americans whilst several of the ex-Warsaw Pact members would provide several thousand 'boots on the ground' to coordinate with those of Jordan, Iraq and Iran.
Twelve Typhoon FGR4's and six Tornado GR4's would be dispatched from UK to Cyprus. Fifteen F-16's from Holland and fifteen Typhoons from Germany would join the UK Squadron in Cyprus. France would order the aircraft carrier Charles De Gaulle with it's complement of fifteen Rafales to sail to the Persian Gulf from it's present position in the Mediterranean.
The full membership of NATO fully agreed with President O'Shea's prognosis of the extent of the growing IC threat and that it should be dealt with now rather than later.
The members left the conference having delivered a brief press conference and returned to their respective capitals.

On hearing the news of the International coalition being drawn up against his Caliphate, Al-Malouf grew concerned of the strength of his adversaries so felt it time to unleash his determination to resist any onslaught. He called for his Council to join him in the control room of the Dam. They

conversed for a few minutes before he ordered,
" Blow the Dam now!"
The rest of that day was taken up with the strategically placing of several tons of HE (High Explosive) that had been taken from Mosul. As the evening sun was settling on the horizon and all of the militants safely off the Dam, all was ready,
"Blow!!!" ordered Al-Malouf.
There were some twenty or so individual explosions which made the ground shudder with the force of a 4 on the Richter scale.
A copious amount of dust, debris and black smoke reached high into the darkening sky, but the Dam stood still. Two minutes passed..nothing. Then suddenly the Dam shook, a bit of masonry fell to the river below. Then a bit more and more then whoooosh! Out poured the water with the power of a billion tons of water behind it creating a five hundred foot cascade of water and mist.

It was early evening when the forty foot high tsunami of the Tigris hit the town of Mosul virtually wiping it clear of the map but it was several hours later that it hit Baghdad.
The haunting Azan early morning call to

prayer could be heard gently wailing over the city from the many minarets. The city was at peace as many of it's souls began to rise from their beds, until the Tigris tsunami struck. It had lost several feet in height during it's long five hundred mile journey down from Mosul but the twenty foot wave ploughed through the centre of the war torn city pouring over the banks and extending it's reach way into the suburbs of the city. With the power of millions of tons of water behind it only the strongest of buildings could withstand the enormous pressure exerted on them. Many just collapsed like a pack of cards. Cars, lorries, buses and what people who were in the streets were picked up and tossed about as if they were made of paper. Buildings collapsed, bridges torn from their foundations and trees uprooted. The water just kept on tracking downstream eventually to end up in the Persian Gulf.

The devastation to Baghdad had to be seen to be believed. Virtually the whole city was resting under ten to fifteen feet of dirty, rubbish filled water with bodies floating at every corner. By midday, beneath the calm glistening water purporting to be a lake, lay nearly seven hundred thousand dead. Added to the total devastation of Mosul this

was a disaster on a grand scale, that would eventually shock the world.
There was not a corner of the globe that had not been heralded of the news by it's local media of newspaper, television and of course the internet.

The effort so bravely fought by the American pilots and Kurdistan/Iranian soldiers to save Mosul Dam and it's consequent action, had been in vane.
The distraught O'Shea was sinking low in his resolve. What did he and his NATO colleagues have to do to stop this madman?
The grandeur of the atrocity in Iraq angered those of the Islamic world, who had not yet seen fit to display an open opinion on the formation of the Caliphate, to such an extent that they now publicly condemned the IC. The majority of the Muslim world were now of one accord in that they would not sanction this behaviour in the name of Islam.
The same could not be attributed to those of a terroristic tendency. Many throughout the world sympathised with the formation of the Caliphate but did not quite have enough spirit to join but on hearing of the NATO commitment to destroy it, managed to persuade many thousands of them to make

good their loyalty. Trails across the world became awash with these volunteers heading for Syria and Iraq wishing to partake in the frey.

It would take several days, if not a week or two, for the NATO coalition to get their forces in position, fully armed and familiarised with the local terrain and targets for combat. Al-Malouf knew that. With the possession of such knowledge and awareness of the numbers en-route to join his cause, he decided to move his considerable force on the offensive .. to Baghdad itself. Realising it's demise and anticipating the chaos that must been reigning there Al-Malouf saw Baghdad fit for taking. It would only take his forces a day or two the cover the distance which would allow time for the waters to dissipate.

The American high altitude U-2's monitored the southerly track of the IC army so fed with this intel Admiral Logan altered the next sortie of F-18 attacks to be from high altitude well out of the range of hand held RPG's. Bombing from height would render the napalm bombs of little use due to their inaccuracy so the pilots were ordered to fit

four Mk82 five hundred pounders to each of their aircraft.
As before a wave of six aircraft left the carrier for northern Iraq.
Expecting further drops from the American aircraft AL-Malouf had the strategic sense to string out his forces over a vast area so rendering any bombing relatively ineffectual. This proved correct as over the next two days wave after wave of F-18's unleashed their ordnance but to very little overall effect to the fast moving army beneath.

"Baghdad must not fall!" shouted O'Shea thumping the desk as he was being updated on the relentless progress of the IC army, *"Get the British involved now! before it's too late!"* he continued shouting at his Chiefs of Staff.
"They will be flying their Typhoons in the morning alongside the Dutch Sir" replied the Air Chief.
"Not a moment to soon" spoke O'Shea.

Another bright blue morning was the order of the day over RAF Akrotiri in Cyprus as the powerful Typhoons rolled towards the runway closely followed by the six F-16's of the Dutch Air Force. The noise was

horrendous as the twelve aircraft thundered down the runway on full afterburners to get airbourne. Their route would take them down over northern Israel and Jordan and into Iraq. Their time over the target area would be extremely limited if they were not going to call for a mid-air refuel.
The enlargement of the bombing force did not go unnoticed by Al-Malouf as his forces were approaching the northern outskirts of Baghdad which encouraged him to enter the city far quicker than he had originally planned. Even by his most relaxed calculations the Iraqi opposition was pitifully small. The water damage had severely under minded the Iraqi's ability to mobilize it's tanks and aircraft. Mostly water impregnation into the diesel tanks of the tanks and aircraft bowsers had immobilised the mechanical strength to fight. With his array of captured tanks, anti-tank rockets, troop carriers and Humvies plus thousands of AK-47's Al-Malouf proceeded through the streets of Iraq's capital city. Another tactic he used was that of loudly broadcasting an offer to all Iraqi Shia's. Should they be prepared to switch from Shia to Sunni and join his Caliphate he would spare their execution by beheading. This proved the most powerful

and effective weapon in his arsenal!

The frustrated NATO pilots circling overhead realised their ability to strike at IC was now severely limited if innocent Iraqi civilians were not to be caught in the action.
The sacking of the huge city of Baghdad took little effort by the barbarous IC who spared no mercy to either men, women or children not willing to convert. Never before had this fabled city seen so much inhuman, barbaric behaviour. Much of the Iraqi army fought to the best of their ability but there was just not sufficient fire in their bellies, possibly from being so tired of war and man-made disasters, to resist the relentless bloodthirsty hoards hell bent on building their Caliphate.
By the end of that day most of the city was under Al-Malouf's direct control.
It was then that the mass execution of those Shi'a's not willing to submit to the alternative will of the sword took place on a grand scale in public. Hundreds and hundreds, mainly the males, were lined up on the oval Firdos Square located near the river and without ceremony needlessly beheaded.
The women and children were marched out of the city limits to a vast section of wasteland in Seaidya where JCB diggers had

excavated an enormous pit into which they were forced to climb before being buried alive!
The stench of death and degradation hung over the city like the 'Black Death' must have way back in European history.
With the capital city fallen Al-Malouf and his close Council arranged for all his IC forces to gather in Great Celebration Square for an announcement. If only the NATO coalition had been given notice of this gathering then a few well placed bombs would have eliminated the IC threat for good ......but they had not. The U2's constantly surveying from above recorded the mass movement towards the Square but there was just not enough time to mount an air-strike. An opportunity missed!
Al-Malouf mounted the hastily constructed stage aptly positioned under the southerly Arch of Triumph (Swords of Qadisiyah) and addressed his following,
"My Brothers. We have come far in such a short time and with us now holding Baghdad I now announce that the country of Iraq and our holdings in Syria will be renamed as The Caliphate."
With the raising of his hands the gathering went wild with delight shouting, jumping up

and down and letting off countless rounds from their AK's into the air.

The coalition army of Jordanian, Iranian and ex Warsaw pact countries had taken too much time to assemble in southern Turkey to hinder any plans of the fast moving IC army. They would march onto Baghdad from the north virtually following the route of
Al-Malouf when he left Mosul Dam and confront Malouf there .....or so they thought!
Al-Malouf had other ideas.
With his ranks now swollen to around a quarter of a million men and his armoury bursting with American tanks and ground-to-air missile stocks and the land of Iraq at his mercy ... he felt invincible.
...invincible enough to march on the vast country of Shi'ah Iran, his greatest enemy.
No ordinary military commander in charge of his senses would consider undertaking such a monumental feat with such limited resources but then they did not feel the divine comfort of a religious blanket around them.
Having carefully considered the territory
Al-Malouf elected to break through into Iran just west of Eslamadad and then onto Arak through the lower northern foothills of the

Zagros Mountains. His ultimate goal would be that of the city of Qom equidistant between Arak and the capital of Tehran.
For many years the west and Israel have been fully aware of the nuclear research facility at Qom. The work undertaken at this highly secret Iranian establishment had long been estimated. The Iranian Government had always been insistent that the nuclear research was for the generation of electricity but western intelligence were convinced that nuclear weapons were being covertly developed. Aftereall it was in 2011 when the then President publicly vowed to wipe the state of Israel of the map! Al-Malouf wanted to get his hands on whatever could be gathered to construct a few 'dirty bombs'! With these, or the pretence of these, in his possession there would be no telling as to what power he might yield then!
News of the onward march of the coalition force reached Baghdad leaving no option than for IC to proceed into Iran with immediate haste. Al-Malouf ordered around a quarter of his ever enlarging force to stay and defend Baghdad to the last man if necessary. This would give his main force time to progress into Iran and manage whatever the Iranians would throw at him.

Anticipating a combined ariel assault from the coalition and Iran he strategically placed all of the captured surface-to-Air missiles throughout his strung out mobile army.

Intelligence reports of the fall of Baghdad and onward push into the territory of their sworn enemy of Iran had filtered down to what was left of the Brotherhood Council in Cairo who were hurriedly putting together an armed ground force to head across the Sinai Desert to take advantage of whatever panic must be spreading throughout Israel. Egypt had been well aware of the dangerous fragility between the two countries so decided that an attack upon Israel from their south at this time of uncertainty and confusion would stand a chance of being successful. Many of the Egyptian force would team up with what might be left of Hamas in Garza and provide a secondary attack to Israel's west.
The middle east was now in complete turmoil. Virtually every country within the region together with western Europe and the United States were involved in conflict.

Could this be the start of world war three?

Russia was heavily involved with her own internal strife so thankfully kept clear of the Middle-East .. for the time being!

As soon as the U-2's detected IC's move east into Iran the coalition prepared to unleash it's full weight of available aircraft. Squadrons of Typhoons, F-16's and Rafales joined with Iranian MIG 29's and F-4's for the ariel bombardment of the IC force.

Chapter Eleven

... The Truth is Uncovered

The first wave of aircraft to engage IC over Iranian territory consisted of five Iranian MIG 29's based at Mehrabad, five British Typhoons and five Dutch F-16's coming in from Cyprus with the second wave of five

Iranian F-4's from Hamedan, five French Rafales from their Gulf carrier, five US F-18's from their Gulf carrier and five Australian F-18's based in UAE following fifteen minutes behind.
Having been briefed that IC might well have acquired several hundred American FIM-92 Stinger shoulder operated ground to air missiles from the captured Iraqi stockpile the pilots and navigators of the strike force would be on their utmost guard. All knew of the fate that befell their comrades at Mosul Dam just a few days earlier.

It was agreed that the first wave of the attack would be at low level with the second at altitude. This might help to confuse the ground forces and Stinger settings. Napalm and five hundred pounders would be slung under the Typhoons and F-16's whilst the MIGs would be fitted with pure five hundred pound bombs. The later F-18's and Rafales would have precision guided bombs for specific targets such as tanks whilst the elderly Iranian F-4's would be equipped with five hundred pounders again.

IC had made good progress in the undulating Zagros foothills meeting almost no

opposition from Iranian ground forces. Unbeknown to Al-Malouf the Iranians were massing the bulk of their army on the western plains of Tehran ready to finish off what remained of the IC army that escaped the air onslaught.
As the British Typhoons screamed in low and fast from the west holding their nerve before unleashing their ordnance on the leading edge of the IC force. The Dutch F-16's hit the rear guard thus avoiding flying debris and flames caused by the British aircraft. The MIG's would take up the rear of the first wave dropping their bombs on areas not touched by the British or Dutch.
The scene around the foothills was one of pure devastation for the IC force as they had not expected such a fast engagement. None of the jets took any hits and returned for their home bases. The same could not be said of the second wave as multitudes of Stingers left their cages with many making contact with their high altitude prey.
At least seven aircraft were brought down with all pilots and navigators managing to eject. Unfortunately the large descending white parachutes made it easy for IC militants to locate those hanging from and where they had landed. Thirteen aircrew

from all four countries of the second wave were taken prisoner. Six from Iran, one from France, four from US and two from Australia. The first contact had been made. Al-Malouf, who himself had taken some shrapnel in the left leg, lay on the ground unable to move was assisted up to be able to survey the chaotic scene.

Prime Minister Benayoun had called an emergency cabinet meeting on being told of the incursion into Iran. All Chiefs of Staff were also ordered to be present for the morning briefing at which Benayoun sought how the best interests of Israel might be obtained from the fast moving events. Most of the military men in the room were of one accord which was of that to take advantage of Iran's eye looking in a different direction than Israel and send in several Squadrons of F-15's to take out the nuclear facilities of Qom and Natanz.
However it took the diplomatic approach of Benayoun and the Deputy Prime Minister to point out that the United States and NATO coalition had obviously formed an alliance with Iran for the destruction of IC and that an attack on Iran at this point could be seen that Israel now supported the actions of IC!

They would have to think again.
Benayoun had no idea of what was about to hit Israel from the south!

Two and a half thousand miles to the west of Iraq in a remote spot in the Algerian Sahara some ninety five miles to the south west of Adrar, the camel train of six Tuareg nomads en-route from Bardj Moktar in Mali to Bechar on the Algerian /Moroccan border broke camp carrying their somewhat elicit sackfuls of Hashish destined for the European market. This long and arduous journey across some of the most inhospitable landscape on earth was the lifestyle of these nomadic Berber tribesmen. They knew nothing else than long distance trading especially in profitable goods.
It had been almost a week since Ahmed and his group had departed from Mali and were very settled in their desert trekking routine. They broke camp at dawn as the long shadows shortened in the soft pink sunlight.
Having donned their Gandouras and until the cold morning temperature rises, their Burnous coats, the six tribesmen mounted their trusty 'ships of the desert' and

proceeded on their north-westerly course.
As the day carried forward the temperature rose dramatically to a scorching forty eight degrees. Progress had been good but ahmed considered a short break for water was necessary but before doing so decided to survey the monotonous, undulating landscape of sand for any familiar landmarks to assist in navigation. Raising the binoculars Ahmed gradually ran the grid lines across the horizon. Then something attracted his attention .... a glint. Steadying the glasses and focussing on the glint Ahmed identified something was reflecting the sunlight. He never remembered anything in this area of a reflective nature before with curiosity getting the better of him felt that a closer inspection was necessary. The thought of it being a military patrol ran through his mind. This he would be keen to avoid.
Sufficiently rested the six Tuaregs
re-mounted their camels and slowly made tracks towards the glinting object which they estimated at around ten kilometres. The heat was intense. The sun was approaching it's zenith. The progress over the sand was slow and the object did not appear to grow nearer. Ahmed called for a temporary halt and removed the antique binoculars from it's

case. As the object came into focus Ahmed could now clearly see that it was a large silver tower standing almost vertical in the sand.
Intrigued to establish what this could be Ahmed ushered the caravan forward.
Within two hours they would all be standing at the base of the object. It stood an estimated sixty feet in height but had two smaller, but broken, fins protruding from the it's side. The overall colour was silver with traces of white, dark blue and red paint whilst the protrusions appeared to be of a silver or aluminium colour. The initial surprise was over but Ahmed was now curious to establish the material construction. Gently tapping it with the butt of his knife it was clearly metal and from the dull echoing it was also hollow. Much of the paint had been stripped from the structure by the wind and strewn over the surrounding sand.
Still uncertain of what the structure was, all six nomads started to kick away the sand at it's base. The softness of the sand afforded very little progress as it just fell back into the excavation as soon as it was removed but they did discover were the letters 'LEB' clearly written on the metal. Then it dawned on Ahmed as to what the structure was

...it was the tailplane of
an enormous aircraft!

Fully realising the enormity of their discovery it was agreed that they would inform the authorities as soon as they were within range of the smart phone receivers at Adrar. Leaving the aircraft structure to the mercy of the elements once again the caravan mounted up and started off, heading in a north easterly direction towards Adrar.

Now recovered from the first of what could be several air attacks Al-Malouf reassessed his strategy to conquer Iran. He decided to split his army into two prongs. The first, consisting of the huge bulk of his men and armour would continue directly onto Tehran as best they could absorbing what ever the coalition threw at them on the way, but he and would personally lead a small force of six tanks, one tanker and one thousand men in a different direction towards Qom. His primary aim was to be in possession of some nuclear material as soon as possible, then the cards would surely turn. By only splitting off a small force Al-Malouf was hoping that it could remain undetected with the coalition's concentration being on his main force. Only time would tell. The captured coalition aircrew were securely bound and gagged aboard one of the trucks in the main force ready to be used as a human shield should the going get tough.

Al-Malouf's force being so small could take full advantage of a small mountain pass to cross the Zagros. This would lessen the distance he had to travel to reach Qom. Instructions were given to the tank drivers not to use heavy power settings to avoid the issuance of black smoke from the exhaust which could be seen from the air.
As darkness was beginning to fall Al-Malouf observed the many flashes as the second wave of coalition bombs exploded on his main force some forty five miles to his north.

In Egypt The Brotherhood were frantically building their spearhead force just north of Ismailia in readiness to pour over the
Al-Salam Bridge, crossing the Suez Canal and into the arid Sinai Desert where they would

disperse into a wide formation for the journey to Israel. The southerly airfields housing several Squadrons of F-16's,
MIG -17's and MIG-19's that were spared the B-2A attack were fully prepared to send their aircraft to the front line but had to wait until the tank divisions were within just a few miles of the Israeli border.

The signal strength bar on Ahmed's smart phone began to blink.
"We stop!" he shouted in Berber language as he raised his hand. It was the Adrad police that Ahmed managed to contact informing them of the find, it's approximate location and the letters 'LEB' painted on the base of the tail. With his duty now fulfilled and his conscience clear Ahmed re-directed his caravan back on course for Bechar. It was now up to the police to contact the Algerian military to go and fully investigate the find and identify the wreckage.

It was the alertness of one of GCHQ's most senior operatives, Jim Norris, that picked up the signal emitted from Ahmed's mobile phone after it had been intercepted by an American spy satellite passing overhead and re-directed to UK's foremost and highly

secret communications centre at Cheltenham, in the United Kingdom.
Mr. Norris thought this message with the reference to a tailplane in the Sahara Desert rather unusual so reported it to his boss, Miss FlorenceD'Arcy who in turn, after due consideration, passed the information directly onto MI6 in London.

At first the report did not seem to catch any important eyes until a close colleague of Group Captain Barton happened to flag it up on her computer. 'Silky' Jenkins , as she was referred to in the office, was a clever young graduate recently recruited to the service direct from Cambridge to assist several agents with their paperwork. Her attention to detail had not gone unnoticed, hence 'silky' Sylvia and when the word 'tailplane' caught her eye she thought to check out the code 'LEB' on the International Register of Aircraft held on file in the central computer.
Lo and behold the code was shown as being very recently assigned to a British Airways A380 Airbus. Then 'Silky's' penny dropped. She immediately took it upon herself to contact the Press Office of British Airways to confirm the coding of the infamous missing A380 that had departed Cape Town all those

months ago,

...Bingo they matched!

The location of the wreckage of the vanishing Airbus had been found!
But how the hell did it get to be in the middle of the Sahara Desert 'Silky' thought to herself. In her uncontrollable excitement to tell the world of her discovery she missed an incoming message from the Group Captain who, still managing to hide out and circulate in the ruins of Cairo, had discovered details of the Brotherhood's on-going attack on Israel and was advising MI6.

'Silky's' supervisor could not believe his ears when advised of her discovery and immediately contacted Sir Leonard Foley of British Airways and Prime Minister Feldman. Both were overwhelmed at the revelation but were in joint agreement that nothing, absolutely nothing should be leaked to the press until conclusive proof that it was the wreckage of BA 4674 had be established. To this end it was imposed upon MI6 to accomplish this task.
Barton was given full authority to obtain a

commercial flight to Algiers where the Algerian Air Force would provide an internal flight to Belkebir Airport at Adrar for him and the Air Investigation Team being sent out from Farnborough. From there they would all have to liaise with local agencies to obtain a caravan of camels and guides.

The small IC diversionary force led by Al-Malouf had made good progress through the pass and were on the downward slope towards the desert floor. To their knowledge they had remained undetected unlike his colleagues to the north who were receiving daily poundings from the coalition aircraft inflicting dreadful damage upon them despite informing the coalition of their hostage aircrew.

Barton's Egyptair flight touched down safely in the cool Algerian morning air which was met by a contingent of Algerian Air Force personnel who waited at the bottom of the aircraft steps. Having confirmed the Group Captain's identification the six airmen then escorted Barton to their minibus which in turn transported the group to the waiting C-130 Hercules transport aircraft parked on the far side of Algiers Airport..

At the top of the open ramp was the four man Farnborough investigation team who had arrived with their kit a few hours earlier courtesy of British Airways.
The four engined transport plane got safely airbourne and settled into the low altitude two and a half hour flight to Adrar.

The five man team politely chatted in an excitable tone and got to know each other. It was Henry Duvall, the lead investigator that suggested to the Hercules Captain that they divert to the south west of Adrar and fly over the wreckage for an aerial view before landing at Belkebir. The Captain agreed.
Below them the seemingly endless sea of sand was relentless in it's area. As far as the observer could see was sand and yet more sand in every direction.
If indeed the wreckage turned out to be the missing Airbus what in God's name was it doing here in this inhospitable wilderness in one of the most remote spots on earth, thought Duvall.
"There Sir down there on the port side" shouted the co-pilot pointing to the object protruding from the sandunes. Sure enough, as the C-130 swung to the left in a thirty degree banked turn, there was the tailplane.

Duvall's first question to the team on surveying the area area the object was,
"Jesus! where is the rest of the plane?"
One of the team in his ignorance asked out aloud if the Captain could not put down in this area as they were so close to the site. Barton merely pointed out the size of the dunes and softness of the sand would make that impossible,
"Sand can be like water at times" he continued, *"It can just slip through your fingers like flour. You will soon see."*
The flight onto Adrar took a further agonising thirty five minutes.
The Algerian Air Force had done well as unknown to the team they had organised a camel train in advance of their arrival. As the Hercules taxied to it's resting point in-front of the somewhat rudimentary building Barton could see the line of eight camels peacefully resting on the ground.. The ramp lowered allowing the team and the airmen to unload the gear.
Barton and the middle-aged Duvall were introduced to the tall, weather beaten figure of Mohammed who was to be their guide and caravan leader. Fortunately he spoke a little English.

Water, food, spades, cameras, tents and rifles.. all were checked and found present. With a hearty wave goodbye from the C-130 flight crew and airmen, Group Captain Barton, Duvall and the three other investigators plus Mohammed and his cousin set off on the long trek to the south west.

By only moving at night the army of two hundred and fifty Egyptian tanks and fourteen thousand foot soldiers and assorted vehicles had reached sight of the Israeli border around fifty miles south west of Be'er Sheva. The overall Commander ordered a dig in and assessment of mechanical condition of all vehicles whilst waiting to be informed of the commencement of the air assault from the F-16's and MIG's. He could not risk moving forward until they had destroyed the Israeli's southern airfields.

By the time the deep red sun dipped below the horizon Mohammed had called for camp to be made. Progress had been good having covered around forty kilometres since leaving the airport. With the sun now well below the undulating horizon down went the temperature like a stone. The forty five

degrees had now become no more than freezing point. Duvall felt so cold but the warmth of the driftwood fire soon helped.
The night passed with sleep being a difficult commodity for those who had never experienced desert life before.
Dawn broke with the most evocative blood red sun escaping the shackles of the desert horizon evaporating away the fine droplets that clung to the surface of the tents. Breakfast was mint tea with cornflakes.
Kilometre after kilometre they travelled with nothing but an ocean of sandunes to the fore, to the aft, to the sides. Despite the onset of soreness between their legs with the extensive riding, the investigation team bravely continued on with their newly acquired Gandouras and hoods shielding their sensitive skin from the fierce sun.

The sun passed through it's zenith and gently coasted back down toward the dunes when suddenly Mohammed stopped, stood up on his saddle and shouted,
"There over there. It is over there."
They had arrived. Within twenty minutes all seven were dismounted and strolling around the gigantic tail-fin protruding from the dune.
"It's an A380 alright " Duvall informed the

group, *"and definitely a British Airways one but what is it doing here?"*
With a little hand digging they easily found the 'LEB' lettering,
"Without doubt this is BA4674. No wonder the search aircraft never found any wreckage. They were fifteen hundred miles to the south of here" Duvall stated.

It was Barton who suggested they camp for the night and commence the investigation at first light. All agreed and sat down whilst Mohammed and his cousin prepared another campfire and started the cooking.
All night the team sat prophesying what circumstances could have prevailed for the aircraft to have travelled so far off course and without being tracked. Pilot suicide, electrical failure, hijack even alien intervention were discussed. They even took bets on the explanation! Barton's theory was that of an attempted hijack that went wrong. Duvall's was electrical/computer error whilst his colleagues held out for a navigation fault. In the morning the truth would finally be revealed.

Qom was finally within the range of Al-Malouf's binoculars. All he had to do now was to formulate a plan of attack. It appeared that he would have the element of surprise on his side which he was keen to utilise. What he did not know was that his main strike force, which had closed towards Tehran, had suffered a terrible beating from the continued air attacks and what was left of them were just about to encounter their death blow from the waiting Iranian Army. The NATO bombing had deliberately directed and coerced the IC army into the massive jaws of the Iranians, anxiously dug in on the outskirts of the town of Saveh.

As the militants drew close to the defence line the Iranian Commander ordered the 'open fire'. All hell broke loose on the Jihadist army. They never stood a chance and within the day it had been wiped out. A contingent of Iranian Special Forces known as 'Quds' had been ordered to infiltrate the battlescene and as best they could to rescue the captured aircrew. This was not to prove successful.

After a careful consideration and exploratory recon Al-Malouf decided upon a night approach by his the troops with the tanks close behind ready to open up when they finally met opposition. So all he had to do now was to wait for darkness to fall.

Duvall wasted no time once the sun had risen casting it's ashen light onto the monolith. Soon two of his colleagues joined him in the digging around the base of the metal structure. They found it very hard work as fresh soft sand just kept falling into where they had previously cleared but eventually after a couple of hours their persistence paid off.
"I have it folks. I have the handle!" shouted one of the investigators as he scrambled away the final offerings of sand with his bare hands to expose the complete door.
The whole team, including the Group Captain, stood around the clearing anxiously awaiting the investigator to open the rear entry door of the Airbus.
Pulling the recessed handle and turning it to the right released the internal retaining bolts allowing the operator to pull the door outwards and swing it parallel to the fuselage.

"Oh my God the smell!" shouted the investigator holding his hands firmly over his mouth and nose as he attempted to climb out of the pit. Then the odour caught the rest of the group sending them scurrying away.

The overpowering stench of rotting flesh was enough to down the strongest of men! Fortunately the Farnborough kit contained several biological facemasks (standard issue when dealing with putrid bodies.). These the team secured over their heads and put on gloves before attempting to enter the body of the aircraft.
The estimated angle at which the Airbus was buried in the sand was in the order of forty five degrees so as a precaution each of those who was about to enter the cabin wore a safety rope around his waist, tied off to a section of the tail.

Duvall was the first to enter with Barton second. The sight that befell them both simply took their breath away and momentarily left them bereft of all emotion!

The cabin was fully complete and relatively undamaged save for a few overhead locker doors that had opened, a few cases strewn about, oxygen masks hanging from the overhead and meal trolleys caught in the aisle but the most wretched of all was the fact that looking down the cabin all the passengers appeared to still be in-situ and strapped in!

Slowly lowering himself down the aisle, on passing the first row of passengers, Duvall cast his gaze the their faces and the horror what he saw slackened off his handgrip with the result of him tumbling down the full length of the cabin bouncing off many of the seats as he did so finally ending up in a heap at the front of the aircraft.

"Duvall are you ok Duvall. Duvall?" shouted Barton.
"Yes i'm fine. Just a few bruises" he replied.
But then the faces of all the passengers on the bottom floor of the A380 became visible to him. They were all the same ..like those he first saw!
All the skin had peeled away revealing the open muscle structure. The eyes, all the eyes were missing. The arms were in a similar state. Duvall realising that months buried in this coffin would have had a degrading effect on human flesh ....but not like this. Something different had happened here!
"*Any sign of Sevilla?*" Barton shouted down the cabin.
"Not sure what he looked like Group Captain" replied Duvall.
" I will try the upper deck if I can get to it" advised Barton.

Slowly he manoeuvred his way down the aisle to the main staircase leading to the next floor. Climbing the salubrious stairway was easy until he came to the body of one of the female flight attendants unceremoniously spread across the stairs. As he accidently trod on the poor sole, her corpse offered no resistance .. it was an empty shell! What could the surprised Barton do than to continue to the upper floor. It was the same story all the passengers were strapped into their seats. The cockpit was now the focus of Barton's attention. The door was locked so removing his pistol from it's holster he put three bullets into the lock. With access now granted Barton proceeded only to find both pilots were secure in their seats but with another female flight attendant slumped over the central control panel. By this time, attracted by the pistol shots, Duvall also entered the dark cockpit. His extremely high intensity torch beam served to highlight the dust particles as well as the thousands of minuscule green particles in it's beam. This seemed strange to Duvall who could not explain the very faint green glow within the cabin. But the first thing to check was the transponder.

It was in the **'off'** position.
No wonder ground radar did not track it's path thought Duvall. He also noticed several other switches in unusual positions. An explanation of this completely eluded Duvall's aviation knowledge.
"I must find Sevilla" advised Barton as he made his way out of the cockpit and back towards the Club World section. As he climbed the walkway the sight of the distorted faces made him want to vomit but he dare not remove his mask for fear of the smell. He controlled the urge.
Passing through the compartment curtain he immediately saw Sevilla whom he recognised holding the official briefcase. Beside him sat a middle- aged woman .. Miss Yellowstone. On opening the case Barton pulled out the book within entitled '**Peace Agreement**'. They had found it. What the world was at war for was now in Group Captain Barton's hands. The aircraft had clearly **NOT** been shot down. Duvall joined Barton,
"Is that what all the fuss was about then?" he asked.
"Yes,.... but how?" asked Barton, *"how could it have ended up here buried in the Algerian*

desert?"
It was as Duvall turned to climb up the walkway that he suddenly noticed the man sitting in the seat opposite to Miss Yellowstone.
He supported a big frame but it was what was in his hand that caught Duvall's eye and sent shivers down his back with fright.
"Barton, Barton look at this. What do you make of this?" he yelled.

"Oh my God no! No! This could explain everything Duvall. Don't touch it! For God's sake don't touch it!!" yelled the Group Captain who recognised it at once. In the man's hand were two glass files each about six inches in length, one was sealed but one had been broken open. On them were labels which read **"Andrexia 9."**
During his RAF days Barton had been advised of various viruses used in biological warfare experiments and this was the deadliest of them all, so bad that it had been banned by International Law. Barton vaguely remembered that it had the effect of eating the nervous system and skin with lightning speed sending people crazy but in a controlled way before they died. Apparently all this happened within just a few seconds.

But why were they still alive .. it was the facemasks.
"We must get out of here now and seal up the plane for good" advised Duvall.
"I agree but first let me search the man's pocket for identification" responded Barton. Removing the wallet from the man's inside pocket they both hurriedly made their way towards the rear entrance door.
Suddenly there was a cry,

"Doctor Duvall come quick we have a problem out here!" screamed one of the remaining investigators.
"Do not remove your masks! Do you understand. Do not remove them!" shouted Duvall.
As Barton left the aircraft he turned and closed the door behind him making certain that the lock handle was in place.
"We must seal this lock before we go" he advised.
"Over here Doctor" beckoned the investigator pointing at their two Berber guides. They were both lying in the sand.. dead. There had been no masks for them!
"Let's get out of here fast" said Barton *"and do not take off your masks for at least the next hour"* he continued.

Quickly covering the bodies with a layer of sand and leaving their equipment to the desert all five mounted their camels and set off re-tracing their original tracks with as much speed as possible.
The early afternoon desert heat made it difficult for the team to breath inside their masks which were now running with condensation down the inside of the visor. The sweat on the men's faces was pouring down their necks. The desire to remove their masks became overwhelming but Barton used his authority to force them to resist. What distance away from the aircraft would be considered safe? Even Barton had no idea. Onward the Farnborough team wandered trying to re-trace their footprints of the day before but finding it difficult to see through the condensation. Duvall, the eldest member of the team, was the first to fall from his beast landing in an ungainly heap on the soft sand.
"Your mask sir your mask put it back on!" shouted one of the younger members. In his confused state of hyperventilating and shock Duvall failed to realise that his mask had slipped from his face.
The few seconds of normal breathing brought

him back to his senses and then realised he was still alive and well.
"It's ok everyone I am fine" he yelled whilst jumping for joy at having removed the mask. Within seconds all the others followed. They were passed the lethal range of the deadly 'Andrexia 9'.
They all dismounted for a rest and de-brief on what they had found. Whilst the Farnborough team debated, Barton took himself aside to contact MI6 and inform them of the awesome news.
Duvall just could not understand how the aircraft could have landed in such a complete state! This was destined to be one of aviation's greatest mysteries.
Sitting on the far side of a nearby dune he removed his Iridium satellite phone (Satphone) from the camel pannier and attempted a call. The connection was made,
"Good Afternoon Group Captain. What news?" he received loud and clear. Barton spent the next twenty minutes explaining the situation as he saw it laying great emphasis on the fact that it was the released bacterial germ that had downed the Airbus. It was not an act of war!. He also relayed the man's name and address from the driving licence he found in his wallet. It was Jubulani Zikhali

on a Zimbabwe issued licence. With that completed Barton's job was done. All that they all had to do now was to find their way back to Adrar although Barton had asked MI6 to request that the Algerian police send out a search party to meet them.

Upon being informed of the revelations Prime Minister Feldman immediately contacted President O'Shea to fill him in.
Immediately O'Shea realised that he had made a **catastrophic misjudgement** with his **'fateful decision'** to invade Cairo. He would have no choice than to request that the American Ambassador contact the new stand-in Brotherhood Leader and apologise before he himself would have to go before Congress to explain the situation in Algeria, apologise and then resign!
Meanwhile the CIA were instructed to follow up on Jubulani Zikhali and take action if they deemed fit.
The United States was in turmoil when the news of the location of the missing aircraft broke and the full truth released..

Chapter Twelve

...Escalate or Capitulate?

It was now time as darkness had fallen. Al-Malouf moved his one thousand Jihadist's forward. The tanks waited. Without discovery or any challenge the IC force had made it to within just a few hundred yards of the main entrance to the 'Fordo Research Institute'. Then Al-Malouf gave the order to charge. The first resistance was shown by the entrance guards who knew little as they got caught in the hail of grenades. The security lights came on, the sirens whaled, the sleeping security guards awoke, rifle shots were fired.. the attack was under way.

Al-Malouf gave the order for the tanks to open fire concentrating on the towers and upper buildings. Few casualties were inflicted on the militants as they advanced into the main development, afterall this was not a military establishment and they were certainly not expecting an attack especially from the ground!

It took no more that an hour for the plant to be in the hands of Al-Malouf.

The main bulk of the nuclear research equipment was found to be deep underground. The IC leader and his immediate council were but simple souls full of ideology and not that technically minded. In other words they did not understand the centrifuges, the uranium ore (yellowcake) or the water plant and machinery scattered about the factory. They could not find what they could take to be a bomb. The world and in particular Israel had for years assumed that a nuclear bomb was being developed at Qom and Natanz........ but Al-Malouf now knew the truth

.......there was no bomb.

The complete attack had been for nothing and now Al-Malouf was trapped in the middle of Iran.

For him and his Caliphate to now survive he had to think quick for an answer. A simple soul he might have been but a clever strategist he certainly was..he had the solution which he was determined to use to the full

.....bluff.

He would announce to the world his capture of the Research Facility and that he had assembled enough material to construct two dirty bombs! Who could not now take him very seriously indeed as nobody could prove otherwise. Even if Iran had admitted there never was a bomb, who would believe them?
Al-Malouf now felt supreme and immediately made preparations to blackmail the western world.
Once again the camera was ordered into action. The CEO of the facility was brought before the camera and ordered to admit that the plant was in the full control of IC. He was then beheaded as was several other Iranian officials. The camera then swung to
Al-Malouf who again had his face covered in the inevitable black scarf,
"I now have two bombs of an awesome

capability. Do not challenge that statement. I demand safe passage back to my Caliphate and order all Jihadist's throughout the world to rise and assemble in Syria. Should I be attacked I will explode both devices. I need not tell you of the consequences of that!" That will get them thinking he thought to himself as he embarked on making preparations for his journey back to Syria. Using one of the thousands of Iranian laptop computers he had the film uploaded to youtube.

The subject of O'Shea's resignation was the talk on every street corner in the US, all TV channels were debating the consequences whilst Congress concluded upon their decision. They would not accept his resignation, just yet, as he had so much of a handle on the present delicate position. A new face would need time to get up to speed with the details of world events, time they did not have! O'Shea agreed.
Then, within minutes of Congress closing, the youtube video hit the headlines which brought immediate panic to the United States, The Coalition and of course the

Middle-East. The anger and red faces in Tehran refused to be publicly interviewed.
All world leaders took a step back to think through the implications!

Israel's Prime Minister Benayoun was perhaps the most startled of the world's leaders and immediately offered NATO the opportunity of a quick nuclear strike against the IC force before they get a chance to use the weapons they say they captured.
President Akbari of Iran was not going to sanction that and would shoot down any Israeli aircraft that entered his airspace.

The apology of President O'Shea had reached the ears of the Brotherhood Council, who whilst not accepting the apology at this stage, had called a halt on the impending advance onto Israeli soil. In fact the tanks were to withdraw back ten kilometres and dig in and wait. The aircraft were stood down. The nuclear intervention could very well change everything but until Israeli's intentions were known then The Brotherhood decided they would sit back and wait and re-consider their options if necessary.

With the vast resources at Langley available to the CIA it did not take long to establish that Jubulani Zikhali was a scientist working at the Harare Medical and Biological Institute in Zimbabwe whose views on the spread of biological weapons was well known to President Zocomo. It was not known to any outside of the Institute of the plans and future intentions of Zocomo's utter determination to become Africa's top leader and to use biological warfare to achieve that. A quantity of unnamed material had been reported stolen and the disappearance of Doctor Zikhali filled the Harare newspapers. Nobody realised, until the CIA had stumbled upon the fact, that Zikhali had media contact waiting to see him in Cairo. It became accepted by CIA that he was about to expose to the world the manufacture of this lethal agent by supplying a quantity as proof. However something had gone dreadfully wrong whilst he was aboard the flight ... what that was will remain a mystery forever.

Throughout the vast north eastern section of Syria right up to the Iraqi border, furnished with the news of Al-Malouf having the bomb, drew cry's of delight with thousands of hitherto non-disclaimant radicals blowing their cover to show their alligence to the Caliphate. The comfort of having a 'dirty weapon' in their control had the effect of releasing the inner inhibitions of so many Syrians and those sheltering in the country.

The circling U2's cruising on the verge of space had no problem in photographing the mass movement below and relaying the intel back to the Pentagon.
Al-Malouf was back on the move west towards Iraq.

NATO's Security Council was immediately convened in Brussels HQ for an emergency session with Israel, the Sunni countries of Jordan, Saudi, Oman, Qatar and Shiah Iran being asked to attend as working guests. The hurriedly arranged meeting was not a silent or controlled affair with several countries beating the table in anger or frustration. Akbari could only sit and be embarrassed that it was his country's incompetence that led to the NATO meeting in the first place.
Israel again called for an immediate nuclear strike upon the returning IC force.
United Kingdom called for calm and for talking to be exhausted before any more

action.
The United States, understandably, were not their usual belligerent self.
The room was in disarray but the Secretary-General called for a policy to be unanimously decided .... and quickly.
A motion for immediate and unrelenting joint action over Syria was eventually tabled by, of all people, President Akbari of Iran.
A raise of hands was requested...unanimous!.
The motion to attack Syria was carried. It was now up to the Generals to plan the strategy with the greatest of urgency.
However, the question of how to handle the moving IC force carrying the nuclear devices had yet to be settled.
The Secretary-General called a two hour adjournment during which period Prime Minister Benayoun requested a very private audience with President Akbari. They met in one of the private reception rooms. There were no witnesses, no recorders, nothing. This was an historical get together between the leaders of these two bitter enemies but the newly elected Akbari was not of the hard line of his previous counterparts. He fully realised that the world had moved on and those, like the radical IC and others, might well crush them if they did not move with it.

His own country was economically crippled by the western sanctions from his predecessor's era and was keen to be able to trade his oil to improve Iranian life.
If Benayoun could be convinced of the absence of interest in Iran constructing a nuclear weapons programme then there could be a chance of peace between them.
Their meeting continued for around the hour and they agreed they would wait for the recall before announcing their conclusion.
Prime Minister Benayoun stood up,
" Ladies and Gentlemen we may celebrate a new era in the relations between my country and Iran. President Akbari has agreed to let my Air Force take out the remnants of the IC army with a small atomic device whilst still on Iranian soil! I will order my aircraft to prepare tonight as time is of the essence."
The room fell dead silent for what seemed an eternity with this short but very dramatic announcement.
Then the Secretary-General spoke in an usually solemn tone,
"Anyone object?"
Again dead silence filled the room as each delegate wrestled with his/her conscience. The Belgium Prime Minister was the first to respond,

"What could the innocent Iranian civilian casualties be estimated at Mr Benayoun?"

"Very good question Sir" responded Akbari, *" If I might answer it. We can use the natural landscape to help. If IC can be bombed whilst they cross the Zagros Mountains then very few of my people will be affected. Are your aircraft able to be that precise Mr Benayoun?"*
"My Air Force could drop a bomb on a house if asked to do so" Benayoun proudly admitted. Again silence reigned.
Then the Polish Prime Minister raised a question,
"Can you be certain that the captured bombs would be destroyed and would they explode?"
Benayoun replied, *"No and no but what is our alternative?"*
One by one the hands of the delegates slowly rose into the air ....28 in all.
"Motion is then carried. Jacob it's all down to you now. Meeting closed" advised The Secretary-General.

With the Head's of State safely back on their

own soil having flown back from Brussels the military machine of many countries swung into action.

Prime Minister Feldman called for an emergency session in the Commons for their sanctification of the action the RAF were about to take but more importantly for the use of troops on the ground should they prove necessary.
The American carrier, Gerald Ford was on standby with it's F-18's in the Gulf whilst a Squadron of F-22 Raptors prepared from their temporary base in Oman, the British Typhoons were preped in Cyprus, the Jordanian and Omani F-16's were ready and the Qatar Mirage 2000's also ready.
Al that was left to do was for the American destroyer with it's cruise Tomahawk missiles to get final placement in the Red Sea.
All was ready for the final order which came from President O'Shea at 0100hrs the following morning.
The first of several waves of Tomahawk missiles whistled at tree top height from the destroyer over Jordanian territory en-route to their programmed assigned command and control targets in northern Syria. Once the Tomahawks had done their job then in went

the first of the waves of fighter jets, the Raptors which stealthily took out troop emplacements and ammunition dumps. The final wave of the coalition jets then cleaned up the vehicle compounds, training camps, tank emplacements and communication stations. All night northern Syria and western Iraq, which had been designated the Caliphate, came under intensive bombardment. The U-2 pilots gently circling at eighty thousand feet reported hundreds and hundreds of blasts.
The IC army had been taken completely by surprise and suffered horrendous losses.

In the cold morning light the extensive damage was all too obvious but not as much damage that one would have expected from such a mighty onslaught. The coalition's use of high precision weapons did much to limit unnecessary collateral damage especially in built-up civilian areas.
But had IC been dealt a fatal blow?

That same night under a separate mandate a squadron of six F-15E Strike Eagle aircraft fitted with long range fuel tanks left Ramat David Air Base in northern Israel:

Target, IC in Iran.

Slung under the wings of two of the F-15's

were a couple of B-61 nuclear bombs with a yield of 0.3 kilotons each. The remaining aircraft were merely an escort and defence screen.
Flying high at FL 30 on an easterly heading for the traverse over Syria and Iraq the two 'active' pilots and their navigators were excited but nervous as this would be the first nuclear drop since Nagasaki in 1945! They believed in the just cause for their use and further took trust in their Prime Minister's orders, however, the pilots, their Commanding Officer and Prime Minister Benayoun were the only living beings in possession of the 'top secret' hidden agenda. The two F-15's carried more fire power than would be necessary to eliminate the IC army. One B-61 air-burst at a height of two hundred feet above the ground would flatten anything within a three to four mile radius depending on the terrain. They carried three!
The secret plan the Israeli Prime Minister had conceived was simple but so controversial and risky. Once the single bomb had been dropped onto Al-Malouf's army the F-15's would take advantage of Akbari's agreement and continue the few extra kilometres to Qom and Natanz and use the remaining B-61's to take out both these

nuclear facilities.
By the time anyone realised the deception the F-15's would have been out of Iranian airspace.
"Iranian airspace three clicks ahead " the forward navigator declared at which point the pilot lowered the aircraft nose and dropped down to one thousand feet.
"Arm port side" commanded the pilot.

Within minutes just the two armed twin engined F-15's in line abreast formation were at six hundred kts whilst the others maintained their protective vigil at altitude.
"Two minutes to target" the navigator informed the pilot.

"I have the valley in visual. Leader to wingman. I have visual. Apply burner when you see my release and alter to 085" the lead pilot relayed.
"Willdo."
"Tanks visual. Five seconds, four, three, two, one payload gone" yelled the navigator at which point the lead pilot slammed to full afterburner and turned ten degrees to port. The ride turned to exciting as the aircraft broke through the sound barrier and on up to just under one thousand two hundred kts.

As the bomb left it's pylon mountings a retarding parachute automatically deployed slowing down the B-61's trajectory allowing precious seconds for the aircraft to clear before the detonation shock wave could envelope it.
The first indication that the bomb exploded was the blinding white light that lit up the sky for several seconds shortly followed by the residue shock wave which severely vibrated the aircraft now at twenty miles from ground zero.
The shock wave sent to the ground below the detonation would have been awesome. There could be nothing whatsoever left, save for bedrock, for a two to three mile radius of ground zero and with precious little radioactive fallout as the blast was delivered downwards from the two hundred foot air burst.
Al-Malouf and his force ceased to exist, except in an atomic form, and whatever nuclear material that had taken from the Research Centre had been entirely destroyed.
Two minutes after detonation the two F-15's parted company as the wingman altered his heading to 100 degrees. Each had their targets: Qom and Natanz which were only a

matter of two hundred kilometres apart.
Flying time from when the B-61 was dropped would be a short ten minutes for each plane at one thousand two hundred kts. The external fuel tanks on both F-15's, now empty, were dropped to improve the aircraft's aerodynamics and consequent fuel consumption.
The lead F-15 which now had only one B-61 left was selected to drop over Qom whilst the fully provisioned wingman would deliver his full complement of two at Natanz.
"Qom on the nose Skip" advised the lead navigator.
"Ok arm the sucker. Remember ground burst this time!"
"Five, four, three, two, one gone " shouted the Nav for the second time that night. Once again the characteristic bright white flash brightened the night sky for several seconds before the buffeting shook the aircraft now on it's way west back towards Iraq.
Meanwhile the wingman had also delivered his two 'babies' onto the large complex at Natanz and was also on a westerly heading, flying at a breakneck speed.
The characteristic mushroom clouds rose high into the sky as the destruction to the plants was ultimate.

Knowing of the Benayoun-Akbari plan the SAM (Surface-to-air missiles) site commanders at Hamadan, Dezful and Esfahan were on the alert with their 'radar eyes'.

Immediately the report of the attacks on the two research facilities was received all three commanders ordered their home-built Shahin, Hawk and Raad missiles into the air to intercept the retreating F-15's.
The 'light-up' alarm sounded in the cockpits of both F-15s.
"Incoming SAM's Skip, maybe five or six" shouted the lead navigator.
"Going down to one hundred. Call in the help!" ordered the pilot.
High above at FL35 were the remaining four 'birds' who had spotted the SAM launches on their passive radar scopes and were busy activating their many Sparrow air-to-air missiles whilst altering course for an intercept of the SAM missile streams.
At such a low level of one hundred feet any surface to air missile would have difficulty in locking onto it's target.
"*First ones away!*" shouted several of the overhead navigators as trails of small, supersonic and deadly accurate Sparrows

could be observed leaving the F-15's seeking out the SAMs. The night sky was filled with red/yellow trails criss-crossing each other as the many missiles and SAMs sought out their targets.

Boom!, boom,! boom! as one after the other the slower SAMs were destroyed in balls of flame by the highly accurate Sparrows.
No Israeli aircraft received a hit.
Soon all six F-15's had safely re-formatted in Iraqi airspace having successfully carried out both missions and headed by back to Ramat David on a very low power setting to conserve fuel.
On hearing the report of the underhand destruction of the the two nuclear plants President Akbari became incandescent with rage and immediately filed a formal complaint with both NATO and the United Nations before sending a personal, very personal message to Benayoun! For the time being Akbari had other matters to attend to. He would return to the age old dispute with Israel in good time.
The Israeli Cabinet felt safe in the knowledge that no nuclear strike could now be delivered upon their country for the foreseeable future.What they had miscalculated was the fact

that Akbari had been telling the truth all along .... there was no bomb or bomb research!

The minute The Brotherhood Council were privy to the events that transpired in their fellow Islamic brother's Iran an instant religious justification for their immediate move to invade presented itself.
The Egyptian Abrams M1 tanks were ordered to advance.

And yet **another** Middle East conflict was about to commence.

Across the Middle East the day passed relatively calmly. Peace reigned for a brief instant, however later that night the extensive wave of Egyptian tanks moved forward, across the Israeli border into the Negev pressing forward toward Be'ersheba. A division of infantry quietly slipped through the coastal tunnels into Gaza and linked up with the remnants of Hamas and demoralised Garzans.
The Israeli command had not expected the stupidity of an attack from Egypt and were taken completely by surprise when their presence was reported by the security radar

at Ramon Air Base in northern Negev. Several Squadrons of F-16 single engined fighter jets at Ramon, Nevatim and Hatzerium were instantly scrambled into the air and ordered to intercept the advancing tanks.

To the west the joint army of Egyptian infantry, Hamas and Garzan fighters broke through the border fence at Be'eri Forest and headed north east towards Jerusalem.

Once again the outbreak of multiple explosions on the dark ground below drew interest from the American satellites and U2's circling high above the Middle East feeding the intel back to the Pentagon.
President O'Shea couldn't believe that The Brotherhood still had enough resolve and desire to embark upon an attack on the mighty strength of Israel ..fools he thought but then, having only just being informed of Benayoun's disgraceful nuclear double-cross in Iran, understood the Brotherhood's strategy.
A mighty exchange of fire took place in Negev as one F-16 after another dropped it's payload on the advancing Abrams tanks in an attempt to stem their flow. Returning

machine gun fire and the occasional RPG the Egyptians managed to bring down several aircraft but suffered the loss of many tanks. The cover of darkness had been the Brotherhood's friend providing them with an advantage but as the sun rose throwing light onto the battlefield the table began to turn. The pilots of the F-16's could now have clean shots with their forward mounted 20mm Gatling guns which had a devastating effects on the lightly armoured tanks but then were themselves intercepted as the Egyptian F-16's took to the air from their bases in southern Egypt and engaged the Israeli Air Force. As the air battle continued it was clear to see that the training and professionalism of the Israeli pilots was superior to that of the Egyptian as a kill rate of three to one was being obtained. The Egyptian aircraft were also constrained under a limited combat engagement time as their fuel would be running low.

Israeli intelligence had now picked up the infantry advance who had managed to get as far as the outskirts of the town of Kiryat Gat without being detected. A further Squadron of F-16's was dispatched from Hatzerium to counter the spearhead as best they could whilst an advanced Merkava tank division was brought to the field from Beit Shemesh.

Whilst Israel was being heavily involved in it's counter-offensive, several hundred miles north in the newly declared Caliphate the NATO strike against the thousands of arising Jihadists was about to kick off. The coalition Generals , much against public opinion, had organised a massive ground and air offensive with an air onslaught preceding the introduction of thousands of multi-national troops.
At 2300hrs the first batch of Tomahawk cruise missiles were launched from the American destroyer in the Red Sea and the British Astute submarine that had quietly slipped into the Persian Gulf. They were followed by several waves of fighter jets consisting of British Typhoons, American F-18's, Jordanian F-16's, Saudi Typhoon's, French Rafales, Dutch F-16's and F-16's from UAE (one of which was being flown by a female) all of which targeted remaining known control and command positions, tank emplacements and fuel dumps. The hundreds of tons of ordnance dropped that night would do much to 'soften up' the militant resistance for the International ground troops that had

been assembled and would advance into the area from Iraq, Turkey and Jordan.
This auspicious occasion brought together ground forces from Jordan, Qatar, Saudi, Turkey, Iraq, Kurdistan and Iran, all of Islamic descent. No 'boots' from the west were to take part in this part of the war. It was generally accepted that the rise of this brutal Caliphate was a religious problem proclaimed in the name of Isam which could only finally be destroyed with hand to hand combat by an Islamic army.
This was an army the likes of which had not been seen since world war 11.
From the north the Turkish Leopard 2A4 tank division of one hundred units plus ancillary vehicles moved into northern Syria. From the south seventy five Jordanian M60 Pattons made their way up through southern Syria. From the East one hundred and fifty Iranian T-72's entered eastern Iraq to join up with the Kurdish and Iraqi armies and move west. All followed by many thousands of infantry. From the air a Squadron of Saudi and Qatari C-130's dropped two and a half thousand fully armed paratroopers over northern Syria who would dig in and wait for first light.
This combined international effort would hit

what remained of IC from all sides. There was to be no other outcome than total victory with the complete annihilation of the IC Caliphate.

Israel was getting the better of the Egyptian attack having downed around fifty of their aircraft and destroyed a large percentage of the tanks. As the news of the multi-national battle in Syria fed down to The Brotherhood, their resolve for continuing their fight with Israel diminished somewhat, to the point of the invasion force, or what was left of it, being called back into the Sinai.

As the Syrian morning light grew brighter the dust clouds from the advancing tank divisions across the country could clearly be seen by the U-2 Pilots and British Rivet Joint command/surveillance aircraft as they surveyed the events unfolding beneath them.
Engagement between the two sides soon commenced but the odds were always in the favour of one side.
The IC, with what weapons they could muster together with the thousands of raw , untrained and poorly armed recruits, were simply no match for the heavily armed professional soldiers from the Islamic

coalition. The unconnected militants fought hard for their cause but by the close of a couple of month's fighting having received enormous losses, the IC had been pulverised into virtual submission. Those, realising the fate that confronted them if they surrendered, preferred to take their own lives. Right across the area of north and north eastern Syria plus most of Iraq, which had so recently been designated as the new Caliphate was under the coalition's control.

The Caliphate was seen to be finished....... for now!

Chapter Thirteen

...Peace at Last

Several weeks had passed since the demise and containment of IC and the full retreat of the Egyptians back into Egyptian territory. The hurriedly assembled coalition had all returned to their respective countries. All, it seemed, was at peace in the Middle East, excepting the continuing internal strife within Syria and unresolved actions that might be taken by Iran in seeking justice for the destruction of their research facilities by Israel, who itself was on the brink of their General Election.

It took the courage and diplomacy of the Secretary-General of the United Nations,

Robert Kuok, whilst chairing the meeting at New York to call for the reintroduction of the '**Peace Agreement**' whose loss had been the original cause of so much bloodshed.
The vote was cast and carried unanimously.

The next item on that day's agenda was that of

........................**Ukraine**

Pictorial Representations of the Regions in the Middle-East

General View of the

Middle-East

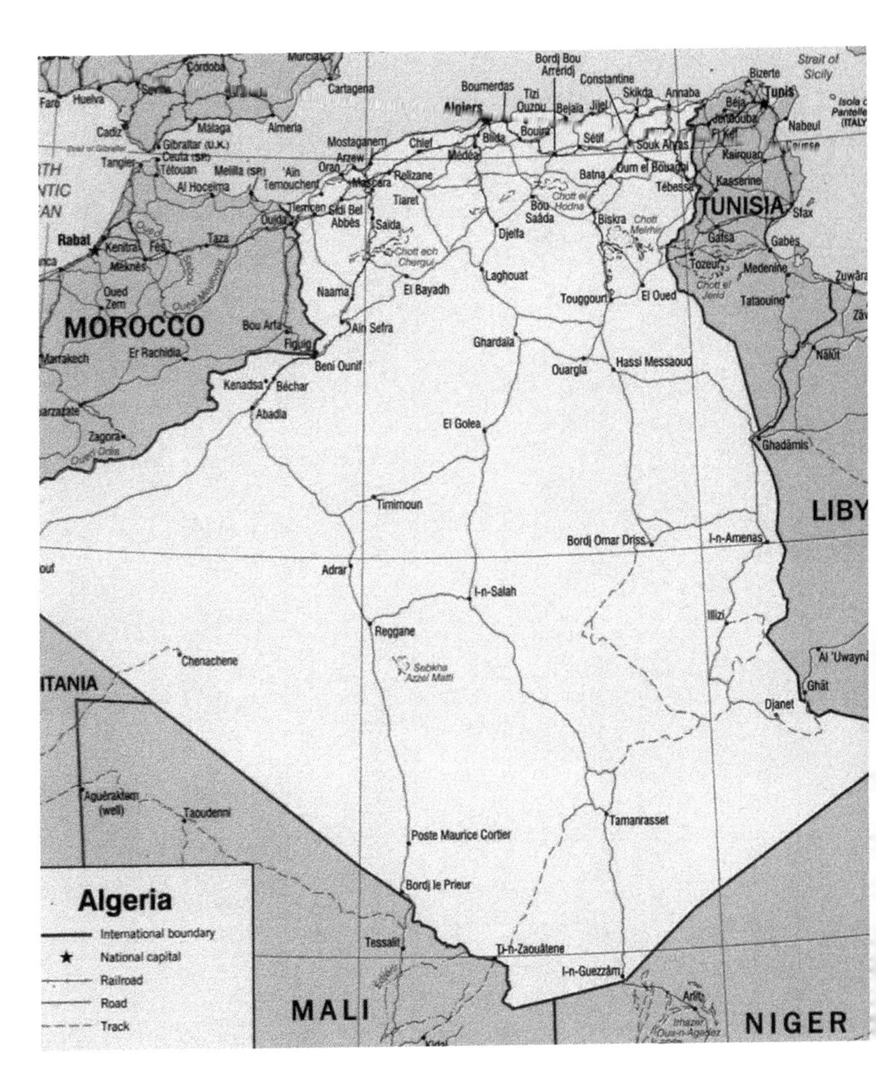

General Map of

Algeria

General Map of
Iran

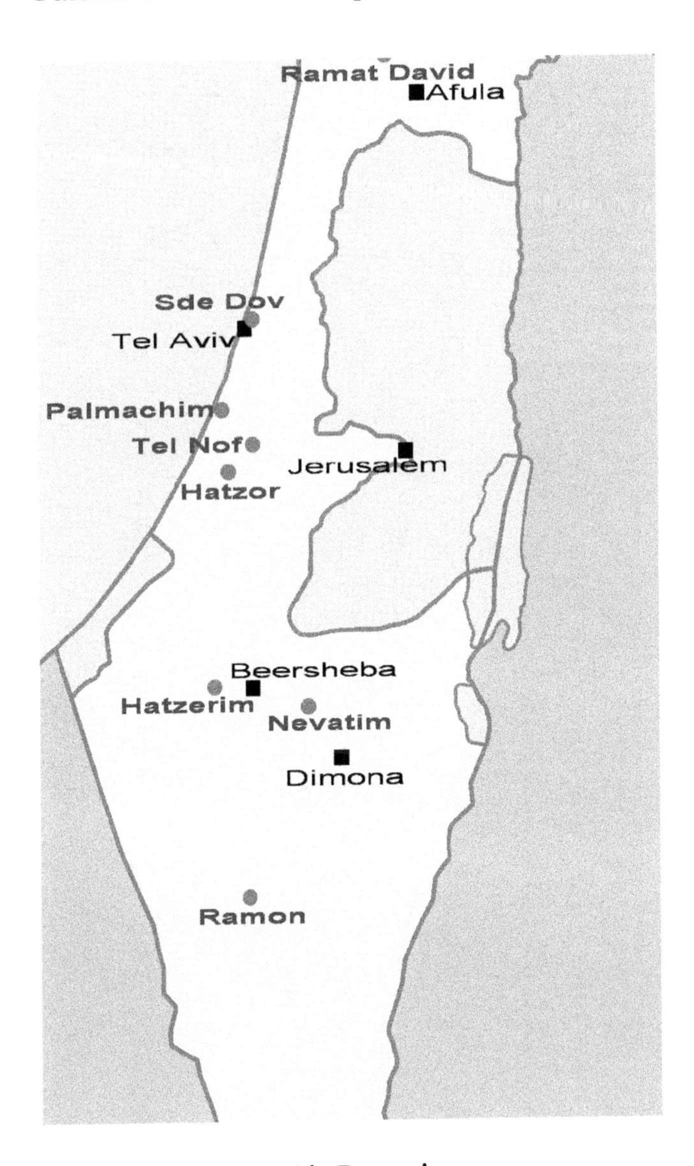

Air Bases in
Israel

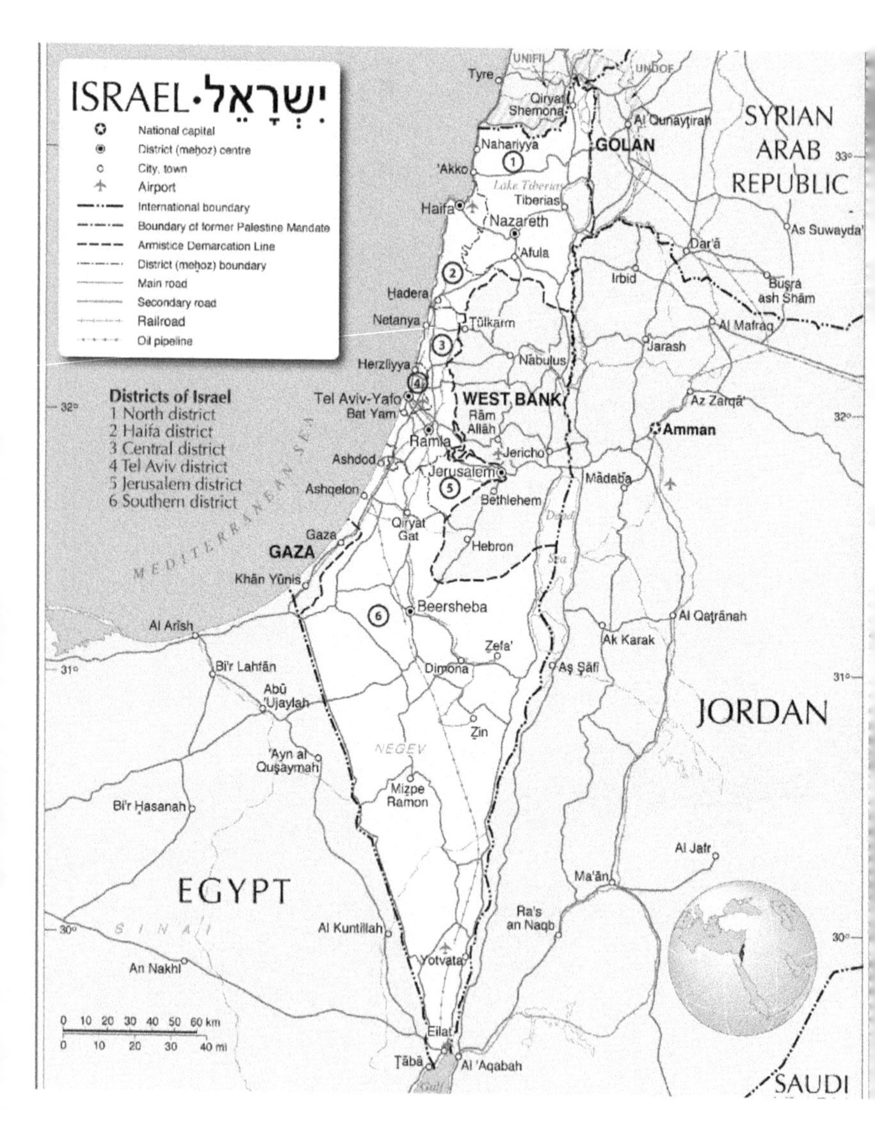

General Map of
Israel

General Map of

Iraq

Lightning Source UK Ltd.
Milton Keynes UK
UKHW051635220119
335699UK00005BA/117/P

9 781320 156592